Mystery of the Midnight Rider

NANCY DREW DIARIES™

Mystery of the Midnight Rider

#3

CAROLYN KEENE

Aladdin

NEW YORK LONDON TORONTO SYDNEY NEW DELHI

ALADDIN

An imprint of Simon & Schuster Children's Publishing Division

1230 Avenue of the Americas, New York, NY 10020

First Aladdin paperback edition May 2013

Copyright © 2013 by Simon & Schuster

All rights reserved, including the right of reproduction in whole or in part in any form.

ALADDIN is a trademark of Simon & Schuster, Inc., and related logo
is a registered trademark of Simon & Schuster, Inc.

NANCY DREW, NANCY DREW DIARIES, and related logo
are trademarks of Simon & Schuster, Inc.

Also available in an Aladdin hardcover edition.

For information about special discounts for bulk purchases, please contact
Simon & Schuster Special Sales at 1-866-506-1949 or business@simonandschuster.com.

The Simon & Schuster Speakers Bureau can bring authors to your live event.

For more information or to book an event contact the Simon & Schuster Speakers Bureau
at 1-866-248-3049 or visit our website at www.simonspeakers.com.

Designed by Karina Granda

The text of this book was set in Adobe Caslon Pro.

Manufactured in the United States of America 0413 OFF

2 4 6 8 10 9 7 5 3 1

Library of Congress Control Number 2013933925

ISBN 978-1-4424-7860-2 (pbk)

ISBN 978-1-4424-7861-9 (hc)

ISBN 978-1-4424-7864-0 (eBook)

Contents

Dear Diary

PAYTON EVANS HAD NAMED HER HORSE after the exact time he was born: Midnight.

I had never seen such a magnificent horse before. His coat gleamed in the sunlight. His mane and tail both looked like there had never been one sleek hair out of place.

And when Payton rode him, she looked just as perfect.

Ned told me Payton had been riding horses forever, and that she and Midnight were first-class champions.

She was so lucky to have figured out what she wanted to do with the rest of her life.

Payton, Ned

Nancy, Bess and George, Dana

CHAPTER ONE

Riding High

"IS THAT HER?" I ASKED, SHADING MY EYES against the glare of the afternoon sun. "The one in the beige breeches and tall boots?"

Ned grinned. "You'll have to be more specific, Nancy. Just about everyone out there is wearing beige breeches and tall boots."

The two of us were leaning on the rail of a large riding ring at the local fairgrounds. At the moment it was crowded with horses and riders warming up for their next class. All of them—male and female, teenagers and adults—were dressed almost exactly alike.

"You have a point," I said with a laugh. "So how are we supposed to know who to cheer for once the class starts?"

Just then one of the horses separated from the others and trotted toward us. "Ned Nickerson? Is that you?" the rider called.

Ned waved. "Hi, Payton! It's good to see you again."

"You too." Payton halted her horse in front of us and smiled shyly. She was about sixteen, with a slender build and delicate features that made her look tiny atop her horse, an enormous bay with a splash of white on its forehead.

"Payton, this is my girlfriend, Nancy Drew," Ned said. "Nancy, this is Payton Evans."

"Nice to meet you," I said. "Your horse is beautiful."

"Thanks." Payton leaned forward to give the horse a pat on its gleaming neck. "He's actually not mine, though. I'm riding him for my trainer—he's one of her sale horses. He's still a little green, but he's coming along."

"Green?" Ned raised an eyebrow. "Looks kind of reddish brown to me."

I rolled my eyes at the lame joke. "Green just means he's not fully trained yet," I explained.

"That's right." Payton smiled at me. "Are you a rider, Nancy?"

"Not really," I replied. "But I took some lessons when I was a kid. And I never miss coming out to watch this show." I returned her smile. "Even when I'm *not* acquainted with one of the star riders."

I glanced around, taking in the hustle and bustle surrounding me. The annual River Heights Horse Show was a prestigious competition, attracting top hunter-jumper riders from all over the country.

Payton's smile faded slightly. "I'm not the star," she said, her voice so soft I could barely hear it over the thud of hoofbeats and chatter of riders and spectators. "The horses are the stars. I'm just along for the ride."

"You don't have to be modest," I told her with a chuckle. "Ned's told me all about you. He says you've been riding since you were practically in diapers, you've had all kinds of success on the A circuit, and you're super talented and hardworking."

Payton shrugged, playing with the tiny braids of her mount's mane. When she responded, her voice was even quieter. "It's easy to work hard at something you love."

As an experienced amateur detective, I'm pretty good at picking up clues. But it didn't take a super-sleuth to tell that Payton wasn't comfortable with our current line of conversation. Time for a change of subject.

"Anyway," I said, "Ned also tells me your mom and his mom were college roommates."

"That's right." Payton stroked her mount as he snorted at a leaf blowing past. "When Mrs. Nickerson heard I was coming to this show, she was nice enough to offer to let me stay with them so I don't have to stay in a hotel."

"She's thrilled to have you here, and she can't wait to see you tonight," Ned assured Payton. "I'm supposed to tell you not to eat too much today, since she and Dad are planning a big welcome barbecue for you tonight."

I chuckled. "That sounds like your parents," I told

Ned. "So are Payton's parents going to be staying with you too?"

"No," Payton answered before Ned could say anything. A sad look flitted across her face. "They have to stay in Chicago for work today and tomorrow, and then they've got a family obligation that will keep them busy for most of Saturday. But they promised they'll be here in time to watch me ride in the Grand Prix on Saturday."

"The Grand Prix? What's that?" Ned asked.

I rolled my eyes at him. "Weren't you paying attention when I dragged you to this show last year?" I joked. "The Grand Prix is the big jumping competition on Saturday night. It's sort of like the equestrian competitions you see in the Olympics. Huge, colorful fences that are, like, ten feet high."

Payton laughed. "Not quite," she said. "Even the best Olympic horse couldn't jump a ten-foot fence! The heights are more like five feet."

"Close enough," I said with a shrug. "Anything I can't step over myself looks high to me."

Ned poked me on the shoulder. "Here come Bess and George," he said. "I was wondering where they'd disappeared to."

"Bess said she wanted to grab a soda." I noticed that Payton looked slightly confused as she watched my two best friends approach. "George is short for Georgia," I explained with a wink. "But nobody calls her that unless they're trying to get under her skin."

Payton nodded. "Got it."

By then Bess and George had reached us. Both had sodas, and George was also holding a paper cup of French fries smothered in ketchup. The scent of grease wafted toward me, temporarily overwhelming the pleasant horsey smell of Payton's mount.

"Payton Evans, George Fayne, Bess Marvin," Ned said, pointing at each girl in turn as he made the introductions. "Bess and George are cousins, believe it or not," he added with a grin.

"What do you mean, believe it or not?" Payton asked.

I laughed. Bess and George may share the same

family, but that's about all they have in common. Bess is blond, blue-eyed, and as girly as they come. George is, well, pretty much the opposite of that. For instance, Bess had dressed up to come to today's show in a pretty dress, stylish flats, even a matching bow holding back her shoulder-length hair. George? She was wearing what she wore just about every day. Jeans, T-shirt, and sneakers.

"Don't pay any attention to him," Bess said. "It's nice to meet you, Payton."

"So you're the superstar rider Ned keeps talking about," George added, popping a fry into her mouth. "He's been totally geeking out about how you're probably going to be in the next Olympics. Is that true, or is he just pulling our legs?"

Payton played with the reins resting on her mount's withers. "Actually, my trainer tells me the chef d'équipe of the US team is supposed to come watch the Grand Prix at this show."

"The chef de what?" Bess asked as she reached over and snagged one of George's fries. _Well duh!_

"That's the person in charge of the Olympic team," Ned explained. "Mom and Dad were talking about it last night after Payton's dad called to make final arrangements."

"Wow," I said. "So this big-time Olympics head guy is coming to watch you ride? Maybe so he can decide if you should try out for the US team?"

"I guess so." Payton shrugged again. "I mean, we don't know for sure that he's coming to see me in particular. But my trainer and my parents seem to think so."

"Awesome." George reached out and tentatively patted Payton's horse on the nose. "So is this the horse you'll be riding when he's watching?"

"No. I'll be riding my own horse—my most experienced jumper. His name is Midnight." Payton smiled as she said the horse's name. "He's really cool. Maybe you guys can meet him later."

"We'd love to," Bess said. "As long as it's not *too* much later. Because I'm sure Nancy and Ned have other plans this evening." She waggled her eyebrows at me.

"Sure we do," Ned said. "My parents are throwing

that barbecue tonight, remember? You're both invited."

"Oh, right." Bess pursed her lips. "Okay, but that's not what I'm talking about." She wagged a playful finger in Ned's face. "I certainly hope you're planning to take Nancy somewhere more romantic than a family barbecue—or a horse show—this weekend. It's your anniversary, remember?"

"How could he forget? You've only been reminding him twice a day for the past month." I was exaggerating, but only a little. Bess is nothing if not a romantic.

"Yeah. Give it a rest already," George told her cousin. "I'm sure Ned has it all under control."

"Of course I do. I mean, what could be more romantic than this?" Ned slipped one arm around my shoulders, helping himself to a couple of George's fries with the other hand. "Fried food, horse manure—what more could any girl want?"

"Heads up!" a voice barked out, cutting through our laughter. It was another rider—a sharp-chinned teenage girl on a lanky gray horse. The horse was cantering straight at Payton and her mount!

Payton glanced over her shoulder, then shifted her horse aside just in time to avoid a collision. "Um, sorry," she called to the other rider, even though from where I stood it looked as if the gray horse was the one at fault.

The gray horse's rider pulled him to a halt and glared back over her shoulder. "Is this your first horse show, Payton?" she snapped. "This is supposed to be a warm-up ring. If you want to stand around and gossip, do it somewhere else."

"Sorry," Payton said again, though the other rider was already spurring her horse back into a canter.

"Nice girl," George commented with a snort. "Friend of yours?"

Payton sighed. "That's Jessica. I don't even know her that well—she rides at a barn a few miles from mine, and we end up at most of the same shows. I have no idea why she doesn't like me, but she's never exactly made a secret of it." She grimaced and gathered up her reins. "But she's right about one thing—I shouldn't be standing around. I'd better get back to my warm-up. I'll see you guys later, right?"

"Sure. Good luck," Bess said.

We watched her ride off. "She seems nice," I said to Ned.

"Yeah, she is." Ned reached for another fry despite George's grumbles. "Our moms try to get together as often as they can, so I've known Payton for a long time. Haven't seen her in two or three years, though." He licked the salt off his fingers. "Her parents both have pretty intense jobs. Mr. Evans is some kind of high-powered financier, and Payton's mom is a medical researcher at one of the top hospitals in Chicago."

"Wow." George whistled. "Impressive."

"Yeah. And I guess what they say is true—the apple doesn't fall far from the tree. Because Payton's kind of intense herself." Ned glanced out toward the ring. "Her parents say she started begging for riding lessons when she was about three or four, and she's spent every possible minute in the saddle since. I guess it's no wonder people are starting to talk about the Olympics."

Turning to follow his gaze, I saw Payton cantering the big bay horse near the center of the ring, where several jumps were set up. Her face was scrunched up with concentration as she steered around the other riders going every which way. As I watched, she aimed her mount at the highest of the jumps. I held my breath as the horse sailed over easily.

"Nice," Bess said.

"Yeah," I agreed. "I can't wait to see her compete. How long until it's her turn?"

"I'm not sure." Ned glanced at the gate a short distance away. A steady stream of riders had been going in and out the whole time we'd been standing there.

"I guess you'll have to follow the clues to figure it out, Nancy," George joked.

I grinned. My friends like to tease me about my recreational sleuthing. But the truth is, they seem to like it just as much as I do. At least they never complain when I drag them into yet another case. Not much, anyway.

We all watched Payton and her horse glide easily over another jump. As she landed, I caught a flurry of activity immediately behind where my friends and

I were standing. Glancing over my shoulder, I saw a woman striding in our direction. She was petite and deeply tanned, with close-cropped reddish-blond hair a few shades darker than my own. As she rushed past us to the rail, the woman was so focused on the activity in the ring that she almost knocked Bess's soda out of her hand.

"Payton!" she hollered. Her voice was surprisingly loud for such a small person, cutting easily through the clamor of the warm-up ring. "Over here—now!"

Soon Payton was riding over again. "Dana!" she said breathlessly. "I thought you were going to meet me at the in-gate." She glanced at us. "So did you meet Ned and his friends? Guys, this is my trainer, Dana Kinney."

"Huh?" Dana barely spared us a glance and a curt nod. "Listen, Payton, we need to talk—now."

"What is it?" Payton checked her watch. "I was about to leave for the ring—I'm on deck, I think."

"Then I'll make this quick." Dana clenched her fists at her sides, staring up at Payton. "One of the show stewards just received an anonymous tip about you."

"About me?" Payton looked confused. "What do you mean? What kind of tip?"

Dana scowled. "Whoever it is, they're claiming that you drug all your horses!"

CHAPTER TWO

Rules and Rumors

PAYTON GASPED. "WHAT?" SHE CRIED.

"Drugging horses?" Bess whispered to me. "That's bad, right?"

"I'm guessing that's a big yes," I whispered back, my gaze skipping from Dana to Payton and back again. Both of them looked upset.

"How could someone say that?" Payton exclaimed. "It's not true!"

"*I* know that, and *you* know that," Dana said evenly. "So who's trying to convince the stewards otherwise?"

"Who or what are the stewards?" George put in.

Dana blinked and glanced at her, looking impatient and a little confused. I had a feeling the trainer hadn't even taken in Payton's quick introduction. "The stewards are in charge of enforcing the rules of this competition," Dana snapped. "Including the ones about not using illegal substances on the horses. Which *somebody* seems to think Payton is breaking. Just exactly what I need right now to add drama to my already busy day." She scowled at Payton.

Just then I heard Payton's name coming over the loudspeaker. Payton heard it too.

"They're calling me to the ring," she said, her expression still tight and anxious. "I'd better go. We can figure this out after my round."

"Whatever." Dana hurried over to open the gate so Payton could ride out. Then the trainer strode off alongside the horse, letting loose with a rapid-fire barrage of instructions for Payton's coming round. My friends and I trailed along at a safe distance behind the horse.

"Wow," I said. "What do you think that's all about?"

Ned shook his head. "I don't know. But I can tell you one thing—Payton's not a cheater. She wouldn't dope her horses."

"How do you know?" George shot him a sidelong look. "You already said you haven't seen her in a couple of years. What if she's decided to do whatever it takes to get to the Olympics?"

"No. Payton's just not like that," Ned replied. "I told you, I've known her pretty much forever. She's never even cheated at checkers." One corner of his mouth turned up in a half smile. "In fact, once when we were kids our families were spending the weekend together at the beach. We were digging in the sand and found this fancy engraved pocketknife. I figured it counted as buried treasure and wanted to keep it."

"Yeah, sounds like you," George put in.

"Very funny," I said, knowing she was kidding. Everyone knows Ned is pretty much the most honest guy in the Midwest.

He shrugged sheepishly. "I was young and the thing was cool, okay? But Payton wouldn't rest until she tracked down the rightful owner."

"Okay." George didn't seem convinced. "But that was then, and this is the *Olympics*."

"Doesn't matter." Ned is usually pretty easygoing. But when he gets that stubborn look in his eye, there's no changing his mind. "I know she's not a cheater."

We'd reached the main ring by then. Payton was already riding in, her horse's ears pricked toward the colorful jumps.

"Come on, let's go watch," George said, hurrying toward a free row in the bleachers.

A buzzer sounded, and Payton sent her horse into a canter. "I hope she's not so freaked out by what just happened that she gets distracted and messes up," Bess fretted. "Those jumps look awfully big!"

"I wonder if that's exactly why someone started the rumor about her drugging her horses," I said. "Maybe one of her competitors is trying to get an edge any way they can."

"Would somebody really do that?" George said dubiously. "For a horse show?"

"Some of these shows can pay pretty decent prize money," Ned said. "Payton's father used to grumble about all the money he spent on Payton's riding until she started winning jumper classes. That shut him up pronto."

"Really? Then maybe it really was—ooh! That was close!" I interrupted myself as one of Payton's horse's hooves clunked against the fence he was jumping.

"It's okay," Bess said. "The rail didn't come down. I'm pretty sure that means no penalties."

We all stayed silent as we watched the rest of the round. None of the other rails came down either. When Payton brought her horse down to a trot after the last fence, I heard a loud whoop. Glancing toward the gate, I saw Dana at the rail pumping her fist.

"Maybe that'll put Payton's trainer in a better mood," I quipped.

"I know, right?" George made a face. "I thought *Payton* seemed a little intense until Trainer Frowny Face came along."

The crackle of the loudspeaker prevented any further comment from the rest of us. "That was Payton Evans with a clear round," the announcer said. "Which puts her in first place."

A loud curse came from nearby. Glancing that way, I saw a short, lean man in his thirties kicking at a fence post with a scowl on his face. He was dressed in breeches and a polo shirt and had a riding crop tucked into the top of one tall boot.

My friends saw him too. "Looks like somebody's not happy that Payton did so well," George murmured.

"Yeah," Bess added quietly. "I'm guessing he's one of the ones who *didn't* have a clear round."

"He's not the only one who doesn't look thrilled." I'd just spotted Jessica, the girl who'd almost run her horse into Payton's earlier. She was riding toward the in-gate to start her round. But instead of focusing on her horse or the jumps, she was glaring at Payton.

"Come on, let's go congratulate Payton." Ned got up and hurried to meet Payton as she rode out of the gate.

The rest of us followed, arriving just as Payton slid

down from the saddle beside Dana. "That was great!" I said. "We had a lot of fun watching you own that course."

"Thanks." Payton gave the horse a pat, then ran up her left stirrup. "He was really amazing, wasn't he?"

Dana grabbed the reins and pulled them over the horse's head, leading him off almost before Payton could finish with the other stirrup. "Listen, you almost ate it at that yellow oxer," she told Payton. "Looked like you took your leg off. I told you a million times you can't do that, especially with this horse."

"Yeah, sorry about that." Payton didn't argue. "I'll remember from now on."

"You got away with it this time, but you won't at Grand Prix heights." Dana frowned. "You have to stay focused!"

I couldn't help wincing. The trainer's voice was awfully loud, and people were turning to stare curiously at her and Payton. But Payton didn't seem to notice. She was nodding thoughtfully as Dana went on to detail every mistake Payton had made during the round.

"Wow," George whispered in my ear. "And here I thought she just put herself into first place! You'd never know it listening to the Dana of Doom."

Finally Dana's cell phone chimed, interrupting her monologue. "I've got to go," she said abruptly, glancing at the screen. "They need me over at the pony ring. I'll meet you later to talk about your next class." She tossed the horse's reins at Payton and rushed off without waiting for a reply.

My friends and I caught up to Payton. "So when do you find out if you won?" Ned asked her.

"Will there be a jump-off if someone else goes clear?" George added. "Those are fun to watch on TV."

"There's no jump-off in this particular class." Payton unbuckled the chin strap of her riding helmet as she led the horse along the path leading to the barns. "So I just have to wait until everyone goes to find out the final placings."

George looked disappointed. "No jump-off?"

"Nope, sorry." Payton smiled. "But don't worry, there will probably be one in the Grand Prix if you come to watch that. And some of the other jumper classes too."

"Cool." George immediately looked happier.

"Anyway, like I was saying before, we're all really impressed with how you did just now." I gave George a sidelong look. "Jump-off or no jump-off."

"Yeah," Bess said. "Especially considering that upsetting news you got right before you started."

Payton shrugged. "I learned back when I was still riding ponies that I can't let anything distract me when I'm in the ring. I just need to focus and get the job done, no matter what." She cracked a wry smile. "My dad calls it the Evans Edge."

"The Evans Edge?" George grinned. "Love it! But now I need a motto like that of my own." She thought for a second. "How about the Fayne Fierceness?" She struck a pose like an action hero.

"More like the Fayne Fail," Bess said.

Ned and I laughed while George shot her cousin a disgruntled look. "That's still better than the Marvin Misery."

We spent the rest of the walk inventing insulting names for one another. As soon as we arrived at the barn, though, we forgot all about that. There was too much to see. Horses were hanging their heads out over their stalls doors. Riders hurried here and there. Farther down the aisle, a farrier was tapping nails into the shoe of a patient horse.

As we headed down the aisle the opposite way, a young woman appeared. She was dressed in jeans and short boots, with a rag tucked into one back pocket and a hoof pick sticking out of the other. Her hair was a mess, and there was a big greenish smudge on the front of her T-shirt.

"Sorry I didn't get up to the ring to meet you, Payton," she said breathlessly. "I'll take him now."

"Thanks, Jen." Payton handed the reins to the woman, who cooed at the horse as she led him away.

"Who's that?" George asked as Jen and the horse disappeared around a corner. "Your personal servant? Must be nice."

Payton laughed. "Not mine—the horse's," she said.

"Jen is a groom. It's her job to help take care of the horses. A big, busy barn like Dana's couldn't survive without a team of great grooms." She patted a horse that was sticking its nose out over the nearest stall. "So would you guys like to meet my horses?"

"Sure, we'd love to!" Bess said. "How many do you have?"

"Nine, but only four are at this show." Payton headed down the aisle, with the rest of us following. "The rest are either youngsters or taking a break."

"Nine horses? Wow." George whistled. "And here I thought it was hard work taking care of my family's dog!"

Payton laughed. "Luckily, I don't have to take care of them all myself. Most of my horses live at Dana's barn, where her amazing staff does all the hard work. All I need to do is show up and ride." She stopped in front of a stall where a copper-colored chestnut with a blaze was nosing at a pile of hay. "Here's one of my guys now. . . ."

She went on to show us a couple of more horses.

"So which one are you riding in the Grand Prix?" Bess asked as she patted a pretty gray mare.

Payton smiled. "I was just about to introduce you to that one. Come on, let's go see Midnight."

We followed her to yet another stall. Inside stood a tall, impressive-looking dark bay without a speck of white on him anywhere. A weather-beaten man with slicked-back dark hair was running a brush down the horse's long legs.

"This is Mickey," Payton said, gesturing toward the man. "He's Midnight's groom." She introduced us, though Mickey hardly looked up from his task.

"Midnight is gorgeous," Bess said, reaching out to touch the horse's velvety nose. The horse sniffed her hand, then snorted loudly, blowing horse snot all over Bess's face and dress.

"Yeah, and he knows it!" Payton laughed. "He's quite a character. Hope he didn't get you too gross."

"No biggie," Bess said with a smile, reaching into her purse for a tissue. That's one of the good things about Bess. She might look all girly and delicate, but it takes more than a little horse snot to faze her!

Payton turned to Mickey. "I was thinking of taking him out for some hand grazing, if that's okay."

Mickey just nodded, reaching for the halter hanging just outside the stall door and quickly buckling it onto the horse's big head. Then Payton clipped a lead line to Midnight's halter and led him out.

"Wow, he looks even bigger out here," George commented.

"I guess a bigger horse must make those Grand Prix jumps look smaller, huh?" I joked.

Payton chuckled. "It doesn't hurt," she agreed. "Do you guys want to tag along while I graze him?" She reached into her pocket and held her hand up to the horse's muzzle. I wasn't close enough to see what she'd pulled out, but whatever it was, the horse slurped it up eagerly and then nuzzled her for more.

"What do you feed a horse like Midnight?" I asked. "Treats, I mean—like you just gave him."

"My horses love all kinds of treats." Payton gave a light tug on the lead to get Midnight moving. "Most of them aren't too picky—they'll eat carrots, apples, mints, whatever. One or two are more particular, but most horses have at least one or two favorite snacks."

"Just like people, huh?" Ned said.

We left the barn and headed over to a grassy area near the fence separating the fairgrounds from the parking lot. The bright sunlight bounced off the bumpers and mirrors of the many cars parked out there, and Midnight snorted and danced in place at first as he took it all in. But he settled quickly, lowering his head and nibbling at the grass.

I glanced at Payton. She was watching her horse, a contented expression on her face. I hated to ruin her mood, but I was curious about what had happened earlier.

"So that drugging thing was weird," I said. "What do you think that's all about?"

Payton's expression darkened. "I don't know. But it's not true."

"Nancy knows that," Ned put in quickly. "I already explained that you're not that kind of person."

Before Payton could say anything else, there was a buzz from the pocket of her breeches. "That's my phone," she said, fishing it out. "Dad's right on schedule. . . . Hi, Dad."

My friends and I drifted away to give her some privacy. "What's with the questioning, Detective Drew?" George joked. "You think Payton has some kind of deep, dark mystery that needs solving?"

I grinned. Like I said, my friends like to rib me about my interest in mysteries. "You never know," I said. "Maybe it's like we were saying before—someone could be trying to knock out the competition to improve their odds of winning the big-money classes."

"Or maybe it's a mistake," Ned said. "I doubt Payton would be mixed up in anything nefarious, even secondhand." He shrugged. "Sorry, Nancy. You might be stuck just watching a horse show this weekend instead of solving another mystery."

"Yeah," Bess put in. "And she might be stuck just watching a horse show instead of doing something romantic for her anniversary, too."

We were all still laughing about that when Payton wandered over to us, tucking away her phone with one hand while hanging on to Midnight's lead with the other.

"That was my dad," she said. "He likes to check in after each of my rounds to see how it went."

"Really?" George looked impressed. "He keeps that close tabs on your show schedule? I mean, you only finished riding, like, twenty minutes ago. How'd he know he wasn't going to call while you were in the air over a big fence?"

Payton laughed. "Don't worry, I turn off my phone while I'm in the ring. But to answer your question, Dad has an app on his phone with a timer that keeps track for him." She tugged on Midnight's lead to keep him from wandering too close to the fence. "His job is so busy that that's probably the only way he could keep track short of hiring an extra employee just to keep track of my show schedule."

"You sound like you're only half joking about that extra employee thing," Ned said.

"You know Dad," Payton said. "He's pretty serious about results—he doesn't like to miss a detail."

Between her father, her trainer, and herself, I couldn't help thinking that Payton was under a lot of pressure to perform well at these shows. Still, she seemed to be handling it awfully well, especially for someone her age.

Midnight took a couple of bites of grass, then lifted his head and stepped toward the parking lot fence again. Payton didn't let him get too close, once again pulling him back with the lead.

"Looks like Midnight must believe that old line," I said. "You know, the one about the grass being greener on the other side?"

"He wouldn't actually try to escape out into the parking lot or anything, would he?" George eyed the horse nervously. "I mean, I know there's a fence, but . . ."

Payton laughed. "Are you kidding? Midnight could clear that tiny fence in his sleep." Her eyes twinkled. "But don't worry—there's no grass out in the parking lot. He definitely wouldn't be interested in going out there when he—"

She cut herself off with a gasp as something suddenly flew at the horse out of nowhere. *SPLAT!* Whatever it was hit Midnight, leaving a huge red mark on his side.

With a terrified cry, the horse yanked the lead out of Payton's hand, reared up, and spun away.

CHAPTER THREE

Food for Thought

"MIDNIGHT!" PAYTON CRIED.

"Loose horse!" Bess shrieked.

Midnight stopped, his hooves splayed out and his big brown eyes rolling. He snorted, then spun around as a shout came from out in the parking lot.

Ignoring the shout, I focused on the horse. "Easy, boy," I crooned, trying desperately to remember what to do about a loose horse. Had we even learned that in those childhood lessons? Doubtful. Most of the ponies I'd ridden wouldn't move out of a slow walk for anything short of a meteor landing behind them.

Luckily, Payton recovered quickly from her surprise. "Just stay where you are, everybody," she said in a calm but commanding voice. Then she stepped toward the horse. "Settle down, Midnight. It's okay."

Midnight snorted again, tossing his head and prancing in place. I held my breath as Payton took another step. "What if he jumps the fence like she was saying?" George whispered. "He could be halfway across River Heights before we could take three steps after him!"

"Shh," I hushed her. "He's not running amok yet. Let's see what happens."

"Good boy, good boy," Payton singsonged as she sidled closer. "Easy now . . ."

She took another step. The horse tensed, but then he lowered his head and blew out a sigh. Payton caught hold of the lead rope dangling from Midnight's halter and gave him a pat.

"Is he hurt?" Ned asked. "What hit him, anyway?"

Good question. I glanced out at the parking lot, wondering about the source of that shout. Several people were milling around over near the entrance. A couple of them were holding signs, though I couldn't read them from where I was standing.

Meanwhile Payton stepped around to examine the bloody-looking mark on the horse's side. She almost immediately heaved a big sigh of relief.

"It's okay—he's not hurt. It was just a tomato," she reported. "An overripe one, from the smell of it."

"Yuck," Bess said. "Who would throw something like that at a horse?"

"I think I know." One of the people out in the parking lot had turned, giving me a better view of her sign. "Check it out—some animal rights activists are protesting out there."

George turned to look. "Ugh, PAN? I've heard about them," she said. "They let some goats and sheep loose at the state fair last summer. Caused all kinds of problems."

"Yeah, I heard about that." Bess shook her head. "I love animals as much as the next girl, and I hate to think of them being mistreated. But PAN definitely takes things too far."

I knew what she meant. PAN—short for Pet-Free Animal Nation—was a national group that advocated an end to "animal slavery," which they interpreted as everything from using animals for scientific testing to "forcing" cats and dogs to serve as family pets. They were notorious for showing up at events like livestock auctions or dog shows and causing trouble. As a local attorney, my father had helped prosecute them the last time they'd passed through our part of the country. Now it seemed they were back for more.

"Wait," I said as I glanced out at the protesters again and spotted a familiar face. "I think I recognize one of them. Isn't that the lady who got all that publicity last year when she tried to save that half-rotted old tree behind the elementary school? What's her name again?" I searched my memory. "Annie something, right?"

"Annie Molina," Ned supplied. "I remember her. She was in the paper last month for stopping traffic to protest the new housing development out by the river."

Payton wasn't paying attention to our conversation.

She was busy talking soothingly to Midnight, who still seemed tense and jumpy. "I'd better get Midnight back to the barn," she said. "If anyone throws something else our way right now, he just might lose it."

"We'll come with you," Bess said.

George glanced out at the group in the parking lot. "Shouldn't someone report what happened to show security or something?"

"Good idea," I said. "There were some security guards hanging out near the entrance where we came in, remember?"

Ned nodded. "I'm on it. I'll meet you back at Payton's barn."

As he headed off toward the main gate, the rest of us accompanied Payton and Midnight toward the barn. When we got there, Dana was waiting.

"Payton!" the trainer exclaimed, rushing over. "Where were you? You're supposed to be warming up right now—a bunch of people scratched from your next class, so they want us up there stat. Didn't you get my text?"

"Sorry, I was a little distracted," Payton said. I expected her to tell Dana what had happened, but instead she glanced around with an anxious look on her face. "Has anyone seen Mickey?" she called out.

Jen, the groom we'd encountered earlier, stepped out of a nearby stall. "He ran to the trailers to get something," she said. "Do you need me to take Midnight?"

"Yes," Dana snapped before Payton could answer. "Come on, Payton. We should have been up at the ring five minutes ago."

As Jen took Midnight's lead, Payton shot Bess, George, and me an apologetic look. "Talk to you guys later," she said, hurrying after her trainer, who was already rushing off down the aisle.

"Wow," George said. "That woman is intense."

"Yeah." I stared after Payton, but I wasn't really thinking about Dana. "It's kind of weird, isn't it?"

"What?" Bess shot me a look. "You mean that Payton doesn't seem to mind Dana yelling at her all the time?"

"No—that Payton's best horse got attacked so soon after she found out about that anonymous drug rumor."

George rolled her eyes. "That's our Nancy," she joked. "Always looking for a mystery wherever she goes."

"And usually finding one." Bess turned to me. "What are you saying? Do you really think there's a connection?"

"Think about it, Nancy," George said. "How would those nutty protesters even know Payton's horse would be hanging out near the parking lot fence? It's too coincidental to think they were targeting her. They probably just tossed that tomato at the first horse that wandered close enough."

"You're probably right," I admitted. "Still, you have to admit it's kind of strange."

"Kind of," George agreed. "But everything about the big-time horse show world seems a little strange to me."

"Me too," Bess said. "For all we know, people at these shows might make anonymous complaints against the competition all the time. Maybe George is right and we shouldn't jump to conclusions."

"Maybe." I shrugged. "Let's find Ned so we can all watch Payton ride again."

"Here she comes," Bess said as Payton trotted into the ring. This time she was riding a dapple gray horse.

"She's looking good," George said. "Isn't that one of the horses she introduced us to?"

"Yeah, I think it's one of hers," Ned said. "What was its name again? Rain Cloud, maybe?"

A pair of teenage girls were sitting on the bleacher bench in front of us. They were maybe a year or two younger than Payton, dressed in breeches and flip-flops. One of them turned around with a smile.

"It's Rain Dance," she supplied. "She's one of Payton's younger jumpers, but they've been doing great all season."

"Oh! Thanks." I returned the girl's smile. She nodded, then turned back to watch as Payton sent the horse into a canter.

Payton rode a big circle around several of the jumps at a brisk trot. Then a buzzer sounded, and she picked up speed and aimed her mount at the first jump, an airy arrangement of blue-and-white rails suspended between a pair of standards painted with the name of the show. The horse sailed over with half a foot to spare.

"Nice," I said.

"Did you see that?" a loud voice came from a few yards down the bleachers. "She really messed up the approach. Not a good way to start."

I glanced that way. The speaker was a middle-aged man with salt-and-pepper hair, prominent jowls, and beefy shoulders. He was surrounded by teen and pre-teen girls in riding attire. All the girls tittered loudly at his comment.

"Typical Payton," one of the girls said. "She's always getting her fancy horses to cover for her."

"Uh-huh." The man smirked. "Just watch her gun that poor mare to the next one."

Glancing back at the ring, I saw Payton and her horse approaching the next jump. Once again, the pair cleared the obstacle effortlessly before executing a tight turn to the next one.

"She's lucky that mare is so forgiving," the jowly man said, his voice just as loud as before. "If she tried to ride most horses that way, she'd be off at the first fence." He smirked. "At least she can serve as an example of how *not* to ride."

Beside me, I could tell that Ned was gritting his teeth. A second later he stood up.

"Excuse me," he called to the man. "Payton Evans is a friend of ours, and we don't appreciate your remarks. Keep it down, okay?"

The man stared at Ned. "Sorry, buddy," he said, though he didn't sound very sorry to me. "I just call 'em as I see 'em."

Ned frowned. Like I said, he's pretty easygoing. But he has a temper under there somewhere, and the best way to bring it out is to insult his friends or family.

"Listen . . . ," he began.

Just then another girl rushed over to the group around Mr. Jowly. "Hey, Lenny, that new black pony won't let Tina do up his girth," she said breathlessly. "You'd better come before she starts crying again."

The man quickly stood up. "I'm coming," he said. "There's nothing much to see here anyway." Shooting one last glance toward the ring, he stomped down the bleachers after the girl. The other girls followed, with some of them casting curious or annoyed glances in our direction.

"Nice going, Nickerson," George said with a laugh. "It takes some real attitude to almost start a rumble at a horse show."

I heard the two teens in front of us snicker at George's comment. Then they both turned around. "Are you guys really friends of Payton's?" the girl who'd spoken up earlier asked.

"Yeah. Why?" George asked.

"I'm just surprised you don't know about Lenny Hood, that's all," she said. "He never has anything nice to say about Payton."

"Why not?" I asked at the same time as George asked, "Who's Lenny Hood?"

"Lenny's, like, one of the winningest trainers on the A circuit," the second girl spoke up. "Rumor has it he asked Payton to come ride with him when she started getting really good."

The first girl nodded. "But Payton turned him down flat. Now every time she beats one of his students, he totally holds a grudge."

Interesting! My mind immediately flashed again to that anonymous tip. Could Lenny Hood be behind that? Was he trying to get revenge, or maybe just looking to throw Payton off her game so his students could beat her?

"You said that's a rumor, right?" I said, leaning closer to the girls. "That he wanted Payton to train with him? Do you think there's any truth to it?"

The two girls exchanged a look, then shrugged in unison. "You know how it is on the circuit," one of them said. "Everybody talks, and usually there's at least some little bit of truth or whatever. . . ."

A snippet of a popular song came from her friend's lap. "Oops, Maria just texted me," the friend said. "We'd better go."

"Okay." The other girl stood up. "Tell Payton good

luck in the Grand Prix," she told us. "We're all pulling for her." Shooting a glance toward the spot where Lenny and his groupies had been sitting, she added, "Well, most of us, anyway."

She followed her friend, who was already making her way down the bleachers. Soon they'd both disappeared into the crowd.

"That was interesting," I said, wishing I'd had more time to talk to the girls. "Think it could mean something?"

"Something like a new mystery?" Bess patted my hand. "Give it up, Nancy. You know you're just looking for something to take your poor disappointed mind off the fact that your boyfriend is totally ignoring your anniversary."

I sighed and traded a look with Ned. He merely smiled. I might be *slightly* obsessed with mysteries. But Bess was just as dogged when it came to romance.

"Should I start with hot dogs or burgers?" Mr. Nickerson asked as he hauled a cooler out through the sliding glass doors leading onto his family's back deck. "Or maybe we can dig those chicken tenders out of the freezer if anybody wants 'em."

Ned grinned. "I'd say you should start by firing up the grill, Dad," he said. "That thing's so old it'll be a miracle if we don't end up calling out for pizza."

"Very funny." His father pretended to pout. "Don't pay any attention to him, Bertha. He just doesn't understand you like I do." He patted the ancient grill on the hood. "Now, where'd I put the charcoal?"

"Your dad is living it up old-school, huh?" George said to Ned as Mr. Nickerson headed toward the shed at the back of the lawn. "When's he going to join the modern era and get a gas grill like everyone else?"

"Probably never," Ned replied. "Mom already knows that Bertha comes first in Dad's heart."

"That's right." Mrs. Nickerson looked up from setting out a stack of paper plates on the picnic table. "If that man could marry a grill, I'd still be single."

I laughed along with the others. There were about a dozen people in the Nickersons' spacious, shady backyard. George had been lounging on a wicker chair since we'd arrived twenty minutes earlier, drinking a soda and trading jokes with Mr. Nickerson. Ned was helping his mother carry stuff out from the kitchen, and Bess was stirring sugar into a pitcher of freshly squeezed lemonade. Various friends and neighbors of the Nickersons were there too, helping or chatting or just enjoying the beautiful evening.

"Ah, here's the guest of honor now!" Mrs. Nickerson said.

Payton stepped out of the house, her hair still damp from the shower and a bashful smile on her face. "Hi, everyone," she said with a little wave. "Nice to meet you all."

There was a flurry of introductions. I wandered over to Bess and George, who were watching from nearby. "I hope Ned's dad finds the charcoal soon," I said. "I bet Payton's starving after her busy day."

"She did really great today, didn't she?" Bess said. "I can see why everyone thinks she's a shoo-in for the Olympics."

George glanced out into the yard. "Here comes Mr. N. with the charcoal."

"Payton!" Mr. Nickerson said when he spotted her. "You're here."

"Yeah, she's here, Dad." Ned grinned. "And I seem to recall you promising her you'd have a burger ready for her by the time she got out of the shower."

"Oops." Mr. Nickerson set the bag of charcoal beside the grill. "Well, what can I say—creating food with fire is an art, and that can't be rushed." The grill's lid let out a loud creaking sound as he opened it.

"Ol' Bertha's really singing," one of the adults joked.

Ned's father didn't respond. "What's this?" he said, reaching into the grill and pulling out a folded piece of paper.

"Probably ol' Bertha's 'I quit' note," George called out.

Most of the group shouted with laughter. But I just smiled and stepped closer, curious. If this was one of the pranks Ned and his father were always playing on each other, I wanted a front-row seat.

Mr. Nickerson unfolded the paper. There were just a few lines on there, typed in a large, bold font:

PAYTON: IS RIDING FOR THE GOLD WORTH YOUR LIFE?

QUIT WHILE YOU AND YOUR HORSES ARE AHEAD.

AND ALIVE.

CHAPTER FOUR

Taking Note

"WHAT IS THIS?" MR. NICKERSON FROWNED and glanced around at the group. "Is this someone's idea of a joke? Because it's not very funny."

"What is it, dear?" His wife hurried over.

I stepped toward my friends. "You know how you were teasing me about trying to find a mystery earlier?" I said quietly. "Well, I think one just found me. Or us. Or Payton, to be exact."

Payton wandered toward us just in time to hear her name. "What are you talking about, Nancy?" She sounded confused. "What's going on?"

I didn't get a chance to answer. Mrs. Nickerson swept over and dragged Payton off toward the house, while Mr. Nickerson called for attention.

"Something just came up," he told his friends and neighbors. "We need to talk privately with Payton for a few minutes." He handed the tongs he was holding to one of the men. "Rick, can you see about getting Bertha started?"

"Well, I can't make any promises, but I'll try," the man replied with a smile.

Mr. Nickerson thanked him and headed for the door. He paused and glanced at me. "Nancy, maybe you should join us."

"Right behind you," I said, following him into the house.

Ned, Bess, and George came too. "Is everything all right?" Bess asked. "What happened?"

"Mr. Nickerson found a threatening note in the grill," I said. "It's addressed to Payton."

Mr. Nickerson nodded. He handed the note to Ned, who read it with Bess and George looking over his shoulder.

"Whoa," George said.

Mr. Nickerson grabbed the note back. "I think we'd better call Payton's parents."

"And the police, as well," Mrs. Nickerson added.

"No, wait!" Payton's face had gone pale. "Please don't call my parents. I don't want them to worry."

"That's sweet, dear," Mrs. Nickerson said. "But they'll want to know their only daughter could be in danger."

"You don't understand." Payton bit her lip. "My parents are always pushing me to be the best. They wouldn't want me to get scared off by some random jerk trying to steal my focus." She smiled, though it looked forced. "They'd probably trot out that old line about how sticks and stones might break my bones, but words can never hurt me."

Mrs. Nickerson frowned. "Nonsense," she said. "I know your parents always encourage you to do your best, but your safety is more important than anything, and I'm sure they'd agree. Hand me that phone," she ordered her husband.

"But what if this is just some kind of prank?" George spoke up. "Like one of Payton's fellow riders trying to psych her out or something?"

I guessed she was thinking about that girl from the schooling ring earlier. "It's possible," I mused aloud. "Someone from the show grounds could've followed Payton here and planted that note."

Mrs. Nickerson's eyes widened in alarm. "All the more reason to notify the police!" she exclaimed.

"Or maybe you just need to notify someone who might actually be able to figure out what's going on." George pointed at me. "Done."

Mr. Nickerson raised an eyebrow. "She has a point," he said to his wife.

"Yeah," Ned agreed. "There's no point getting Mr. and Mrs. Evans all riled up over nothing. Let's let Nancy look into it first. If it's just some prankster or crazy competitor, she'll figure it out."

His mother glanced at me, seeming uncertain. "Well . . ."

Meanwhile, Payton just looked confused. "Let

Nancy look into it?" she said. "What do you mean?"

"Oh, right." Bess smiled. "Payton doesn't know about our local sleuthing prodigy."

She and the others took turns explaining. Payton listened, nodding along but still looking skeptical.

"Nancy Drew, girl detective—I know it sounds weird, right?" Ned finished with a chuckle. "But trust me, Payton. If anyone can help you, it's Nancy."

"I suppose it wouldn't hurt to give her a chance to look into it a bit," Mrs. Nickerson said slowly. She glanced at her husband, who nodded.

"It's worth a try," Mr. Nickerson said. "But if you can't clear things up quickly, Nancy—or if you sense any real danger—we'll definitely be calling in the troops." He put a hand on Payton's shoulder. "And I want you to be careful until we know what's going on, all right? We'll keep an eye on you while you're here, of course. But you might want to mention this to your trainer, so she can keep an extra-close watch while you're at the show."

"Ned and I were planning to spend the day at the

show tomorrow anyway," I said. "We can help keep a lookout."

"And we can come help," Bess said, and George nodded.

"Thanks, you guys." Payton sounded grateful. "I'm sure this is nothing. Really."

"All right." Mrs. Nickerson still didn't sound completely convinced. "We'll give this a chance. But please let us know if you uncover anything worrisome, Nancy." She stood up. "Now we'd better get back out there before our other guests think we've abandoned them."

She hurried outside with her husband right behind her. Bess, George, and Payton headed out too. I started to follow, but Ned stopped me with a hand on the arm.

"I have a confession to make," he said once we were alone. "I, um, wasn't planning on taking you to the horse show tomorrow."

"You weren't? But I thought—"

"I know I told you that was the plan." He shrugged, looking sheepish. "But I was actually going to whisk you off for a romantic picnic at Cliff View Park instead. You know—for our anniversary."

"You were?" I was touched. "That sounds amazing. Even Bess would be impressed."

He laughed. "Yeah, it was killing me today not to just tell her so she'd get off my back," he said. "But I wanted it to be a surprise."

"I'm surprised." I smiled and stood on tiptoes to kiss him on the cheek. "Thank you."

"But that's what I'm saying." Ned sounded troubled. "I don't think we can go. Not with this Payton business hanging over our heads. I'm worried about her. Plus, you just pretty much promised my folks we'd be at that horse show all day tomorrow."

I cocked an eyebrow. "Or at least all day until we solve the mystery. What if we get there early and wrap it up before lunchtime? Then we could still have our picnic in the afternoon."

That made Ned look happier. "True. Do you think you can figure it out that quickly?"

"So far the most obvious theory is that this might

be a straightforward case of envy-based petty sabo-tage." I shrugged. "How tricky could it be?"

I yawned as I pulled my car into the show's parking lot. It was early—so early that I found a parking spot pretty close to the gate. Spotting a familiar car a few spots down, I pulled out my cell phone and called Ned.

"Are you here?" his cheerful voice asked after just a couple of rings. He's definitely a morning person.

"Just got here," I replied as I climbed out of my car. "Where are you?"

"At the barn with Payton. Mom and Dad insisted I drive her over and not let her out of my sight. They're still pretty freaked out about the whole situation."

"I know." I pocketed my keys. "That's another good reason to solve this mystery as quickly as possible."

"Yeah. Are Bess and George with you?"

"They're meeting us here later. They didn't see the point of getting up quite this early." I glanced around again at the nearly empty parking lot. "They figured nobody would be around to question at the crack of dawn. And I didn't want to tell them why I was in such a hurry."

He chuckled. "Got it. So what's the plan?"

"You stick with Payton," I said. "I talk to some other people, start figuring out a suspect list. I'll call or text if I find anything interesting."

After we hung up, I headed for the entrance gate. Halfway there, I heard someone calling my name. It was Annie Molina, the local activist. She was rushing toward me, her full, flowing skirt billowing out around her legs and her round face cracked into a broad smile. Her PAN cohorts from yesterday were nowhere in sight. Maybe they were sleeping in, just like Bess and George.

"Nancy Drew!" she exclaimed. "It is Nancy Drew, right? Carson Drew's daughter, the one who's always getting written up in the papers for solving crimes and such?" She tittered, pushing aside a lock of curly brown hair as the breeze tossed it into her face.

"Yes, that's me. It's Annie, right?"

"Yes!" Annie looked thrilled that I'd recognized

her. "I just wanted to say hello, and to tell you a few things you might not know about horse shows like this one."

Uh-oh. Here it came.

"I'm sorry," I said quickly. "I really need to—"

"These horses are nothing but slaves!" Annie exclaimed dramatically. She paused and waited for my reaction.

"I see," I answered quickly and dodged around her, heading for the entrance. "Well, thanks for the info. We'll catch up later."

"Wait!" she cried.

But I didn't. I made a break for the gate, easily leaving her behind.

Once inside, I headed toward the barn where Payton's horses were stabled. Halfway there, I spotted Dana. She was riding a large chestnut gelding with four white stockings. I leaned on the rail to watch.

This was the first time I'd seen Dana on a horse, and I was impressed. She might come across as tense and abrupt on the ground. But all that disappeared in the saddle. She looked like a fluid part of her mount. There was a jump set up in the middle of the ring, consisting of some bright-yellow-striped rails with a planter full of flowers underneath. The horse was eyeing the obstacle nervously. Every time he got near it he spooked, jumping to the side and speeding up.

Dana didn't react except to bring the horse back around. Again and again, until the horse was barely flicking an ear at the jump. Finally she turned him and trotted directly toward the obstacle. The horse's ears pricked forward with alarm, and I held my breath, certain that he was going to put on the brakes.

"Get up," Dana urged, her voice stern but calm. At the same time, she gave the horse a tap behind her leg with the crop she was holding.

The horse lurched forward, speeding up and zigzagging a bit. But Dana kept him straight with her legs and the reins. With one last kick, she sent him leaping over the jump. He cleared it by about two feet and landed snorting and with his head straight up in the air. But Dana calmly circled around and came again. By the fifth or sixth time, the horse was jumping calmly.

As she brought the gelding to a walk and gave him a pat, Dana noticed me standing there. "Hello," she said, riding over. "You're Payton's friend. Uh, Lucy, right?"

"Nancy," I corrected. I smiled and nodded at the horse. "Looks like you were making him face his fears."

Dana chuckled and stroked the gelding's sweaty neck. "He's a good jumper, but a huge chicken about certain types of things. All he needs is a little patience and he gets over it. I just wanted to make sure it was now, with me, and not in the show ring with his twelve-year-old owner."

I nodded, a little surprised. The Dana sitting in front of me right now seemed like a whole different kind of person from the one I'd seen with Payton yesterday. But I pushed the thought aside.

"Listen, I know you're probably really busy," I said, "but I was hoping to talk to you about something. Do you have a second?"

"Just barely." Dana checked her watch. Then she

dismounted and led the horse out through the gate nearby. "I need to get this guy back to the barn, then meet a student at a different ring for a lesson. What did you want to talk about?"

I hesitated, not sure what to say. My usual method was to treat everyone as a suspect until the evidence indicated I should do otherwise. Dana was Payton's longtime trusted trainer. But did that mean she was innocent?

"It's about Payton," I said, deciding to keep it vague—just in case. "I'm, um, worried about her."

Dana stopped fiddling with the horse's stirrups and turned to face me. "Oh?" She peered into my face. "That's funny. I'm pretty worried about Payton myself."

"Really? How so?"

Dana unsnapped her riding helmet and pulled it off, running a hand through her short hair. "She's not herself lately. I'm afraid she's losing her competitive edge."

"You mean because of what happened yesterday?" I asked. "The accusation that she drugs her horses?"

Dana blinked. "Actually, I almost forgot about that. No, this has been going on since way before yesterday. At least a month, maybe longer. It's like somewhere along the way, she just lost it."

"What do you mean?"

Dana shrugged, some of that impatience I'd seen yesterday creeping back into her expression. "Hard to describe. Just that these past few shows, it's like she's not that into it anymore." The horse shifted his weight, and Dana glanced over at him.

"Okay." I could tell the trainer was getting antsy. "So is there any chance this drug thing isn't the first time someone tried to psych her out, started a rumor or whatever? Could there be other incidents she didn't tell you about?"

"I suppose it's possible. Payton's a teenager, after all, and everyone knows they aren't always super forthcoming." Dana glanced at me, then grimaced as she belatedly remembered—or noticed—my age. "No offense."

"None taken. Do you know if Payton has any

enemies? Like competitors who might want to throw her off her game or something?"

"Funny you should ask." Dana frowned. "For such a sweet, hardworking girl, Payton *has* managed to make a couple of enemies."

I held my breath. Now we were getting somewhere! I wondered if one of the enemies Dana was alluding to could be Lenny Hood. The more I thought about the comments he'd made yesterday, the more troubling they seemed.

"Who are—," I began.

The shrill buzz of Dana's phone cut me off. She whipped the phone to her ear. "Dana here," she said.

She listened to whoever was on the other end for a moment. Her expression went grim. When she hung up, she didn't keep me in suspense about why.

"Well, that does it," she said. "Midnight just flunked his drug test!"

CHAPTER FIVE

Test Case

"WHAT?" I EXCLAIMED. "WHAT DO YOU MEAN, he flunked?"

Dana dropped her phone into her pocket. "What do you think I mean?" she snapped. "They found a forbidden substance when they tested his urine. Theobromine, to be specific."

"Theobromine? What's that?"

"What do I look like, a chemist?" Dana said. "All I know is it's an ingredient in chocolate, and tea, and maybe some other stuff like that."

I wrinkled my nose in confusion. "I don't get it.

Who would give chocolate or tea to a horse, and why? And even if they did, who would even know something like that was against the rules?"

Dana's frown deepened. "Anyone who shows seriously on the A circuit, that's who. Or they *should*, anyway. I know for a fact that Payton knew. Someone she knows at another barn got in big trouble for letting her horse drink cola at shows. Similar kind of thing."

I almost smiled at the image of a horse drinking cola. But this wasn't the time.

"How does the testing work?" I asked. "I mean, did someone just go grab Midnight out of his stall just now and—"

"Not just now." Dana stared at me as if I were the stupidest person on the face of the earth. Or at least at this horse show. "He was chosen for testing at a show a few weeks back. Takes a while to get the results, and if it's negative you never hear anything. But if it's positive . . ."

"I see." This put a new spin on the case. If Payton was being framed or psyched out, it clearly hadn't started at this particular show. "Could someone have slipped him something with theobromine in it, then set him up to be tested that day?" I asked. "Like the same person who gave the stewards that anonymous tip, for instance?"

"It doesn't work that way." Dana shook her head. "The testing is totally random. There's no way to tell which horses will be pulled at any given show."

I could feel my theories deflating in the face of the facts Dana was telling me. "All right, then who does the actual testing? Any chance there was some hanky-panky there?"

"No," Dana replied flatly. "The testers are mostly vets or other outside people, and they send the samples to an independent lab. Everything's carefully monitored by the USEF—that's the national governing body of these shows. There's about a one in a zillion chance of hanky-panky in the process."

"So you're saying it's got to be true," I said. "Midnight really did have theobromine in his system. How did it get there?"

"That's what *I'd* like to know." Dana sounded

testy. "Apparently the level of theobromine they found is borderline, so there's going to have to be some kind of official ruling made about whether a suspension is warranted. Luckily, our records are clean, but . . ."

"You mean yours and Payton's?"

"And Midnight's, too." Dana yanked her phone out of her pocket. "I need to talk to Payton about this. *Now*. Here, take him back to the barn."

She tossed the chestnut gelding's reins at me. I gulped. "Wait, I—"

It was too late. Dana was already stomping away, madly texting as she went. A moment later she disappeared around the corner of the nearest building.

I stared up at the horse, who suddenly seemed a lot taller than he had a second ago. Definitely a *lot* taller than those ponies from my long-ago lessons.

"Nice horsie?" I said uncertainly. "Um, good boy?"

I gave an experimental tug on the reins. The horse yanked his head up, almost ripping the reins out of my hands. He regarded me suspiciously, then took a step backward.

"Wait," I said. "Don't do that. Um . . ."

"Hi," a friendly voice said behind me. "You're Payton's friend, right? Are you okay?"

It was one of the teens who had filled us in about Lenny Hood the day before. "Oh, hi," I greeted her with relief. "Listen, Dana just left me with this horse, and I'm not sure what to do with it."

The girl reached out to take the reins from me. "That's Dana," she said with a touch of fondness in her voice. "When she gets hyped up about something, she tends to forget that not everyone is there to be her servant." She giggled. "One time my grandma came to one of my shows, and Dana wanted her to jog a horse so Dana could see if it was lame. My grandma's seventy-six, uses a cane, and never touched an animal bigger than her Pekingese!"

I smiled. "So is Dana your trainer too?" That explained how the girl knew so much about Payton.

"Uh-huh. I'm Rachel, by the way."

"Nancy. Thanks for rescuing me." I gestured at the horse, who now stood placidly at the other end of the reins. "I think he was about to take off for the hills."

Rachel giggled again. "No problem. See you later."

She headed off with the horse in tow. My smile faded as my mind returned to what Dana had just told me. As if Ned's parents and my anniversary plans weren't enough, now I had an even more important reason to want to solve this case quickly. If I didn't, and the horse show officials decided against Midnight, Payton could lose her chance to ride in front of the Olympic chef d'équipe tomorrow!

I pulled out my phone and called Ned. "Sorry, it looks like I might need a rain check on those anniversary plans after all." I filled him in on the news about the drug test.

"Wow," Ned said. "That's serious business."

"I know. So did Dana find Payton and tell her? What does she think?"

"I don't know." Ned sounded worried. "I was actually about to call you for two reasons. The first is that I lost track of Payton a few minutes ago."

"What? But you promised your parents you'd stick

with her." I wasn't really that worried about Payton's physical safety while she was on the busy horse show grounds. But still, we'd promised.

"I know, but it's really their fault," Ned said. "My mom called me a little while ago, and I guess Payton must have wandered off while I was on the phone."

I leaned against a handy fence post. "Okay. What's the second reason you were going to call me?"

"Like I said, my mom called." Ned sounded grim. "I guess she was feeling guilty about keeping all this from Payton's parents. So she called them a little while ago."

"Oh." I couldn't say I was surprised. Mrs. Nickerson wasn't the type of person to be comfortable keeping secrets. Especially from one of her best friends. "How'd they take it? Were they freaked out?"

"Not exactly. They said it wasn't the first time something like this has happened."

"What?" I pressed the phone closer to my ear as several preteens wandered past me, chatting and laughing loudly. "What do you mean?"

"A similar note turned up at a show Payton rode in a couple of weeks ago," Ned said. "It was tucked under the windshield wiper of her parents' car after the show. Sounds like Payton's dad was convinced it was just sour grapes from some competitor. He insisted everyone ignore it. Wouldn't even let Payton tell Dana or anyone else at the barn."

"Wow." I took that in, adding it to the growing case file taking shape in my head. "So whoever's trying to scare Payton either knows her well enough to know which car belongs to her family . . ."

"Or is a stalker type who follows her around so he or she can leave those notes in weird locations," Ned finished. "Creepy."

"Definitely. Which means this case just got a lot more serious." I bit my lip. "We'd better get back to work. I want to find Dana again—she was about to tell me about Payton's enemies when she rushed off."

"Sounds like a plan. I'll try to find Payton and let her know what's going on."

As I hung up the phone, it buzzed again. Checking

the readout, I saw a text from Bess reading WE'RE HERE.

I texted back, and soon we met up near the entrance. "Those PAN freaks are back again today," George said before I could say a word. "They practically accosted us on our way past."

"Uh-huh." I wasn't interested in the protesters just then. "But listen, you guys will never believe what's been happening around here. . . ."

Their eyes widened as I filled them in. When I finished, George let out a low whistle. "Do you really think someone could be stalking Payton?" she said. "But why?"

"And is it connected with Midnight's drug results?" Bess added.

"That's what we need to find out. I'm hoping Dana can help." I sighed. "She started to tell me about how Payton has a few enemies, but that phone call interrupted and then she rushed off."

"I can tell you one enemy," George said. "That girl Jessica. If looks could kill, we would've witnessed a murder at least twice over just yesterday."

"Yeah." I agreed. "Jessica really seemed to have it out for Payton. But she's even younger than Payton herself. I could see her leaving nasty notes, maybe. But would she really follow Payton back to Ned's house to do it? And what about that drug test?"

"I don't know," Bess said. "But I know who else should be on the suspect list—that rude trainer we heard insulting Payton yesterday."

"Lenny Hood." I nodded. "I was thinking about him too. I definitely want to ask Dana about him."

"So let's find her and ask," George said. "Where do you think she could be?"

"Last time I saw her, she was looking for Payton." I shrugged. "Guess we should start by checking at the barn."

We hurried across the show grounds, pausing at each riding ring we passed just long enough to ascertain that Payton wasn't in any of them. She wasn't at any of her horse's stalls, either, or hanging out on the benches out front with the other kids from her barn.

The day before, Payton had shown us around the

stabling area and pointed out the tack stall where all the saddles and other equipment were kept. When I glanced in, the place was deserted except for Rachel and a younger girl in riding clothes. They were huddled around one of the saddle racks in the corner, their voices loud and excited.

"Hi," I said as my friends and I stepped in. "Have either of you guys seen Dana lately? Or Payton?"

The girls spun around. "Nancy!" Rachel exclaimed. "Oh my gosh, I can't believe it!"

"Can't believe what?" I asked.

"Come look!" She grabbed my sleeve, dragging me to the saddle rack. "Can you believe someone did this to Payton's saddle?"

I gasped. The saddle's seat had been slashed to ribbons!

CHAPTER SIX

Vandal Scandal

"ARE YOU SURE THIS IS PAYTON'S SADDLE?"
I asked the girls.

"Definitely," the younger one spoke up. "It's practically brand-new, too. Her dad bought it for her after she won a big class at Devon."

"I already texted Dana to tell her," Rachel put in. "She's on her way."

"Good." I leaned closer to the saddle for a better look, but didn't touch it. If Dana called the cops, I didn't want to mess up any potential evidence.

"Pretty thorough job," Bess said over my shoulder.

"Yeah." The leather seat was a total loss. Every inch of it was sliced all the way down to the padding underneath.

"Who would do something like this?" the younger girl wondered, her voice shaking a little.

I turned to face her. "I was just going to ask you two the same thing," I said. "Do you know of anyone who dislikes Payton?"

Rachel and the younger girl traded a look. Then they both shrugged.

"Out of the junior riders on the circuit, it's mostly just Jessica," Rachel said. "Jessica Watts. She's this rider from another barn near ours. She's always super rude to Payton when they compete against each other."

"Or even *see* each other," the second girl added.

"Yeah, I'm pretty sure we've seen her in action." George grimaced.

"She's around Payton's age, right?" I said. "Brown hair, narrow chin, rides a tall gray horse?"

"That's her," Rachel confirmed.

"Why doesn't she like Payton?" Bess asked.

"We don't know," Rachel said, as the other girl nodded. "Probably just because Payton usually beats her, I guess."

"Does Jessica hate Payton enough to do something like this?" George waved a hand at the ruined saddle.

Rachel glanced at it, looking dubious. "I don't know. I always thought she was just kind of snotty. But you never know, I guess."

A thought occurred to me. "That big jumper class Payton won—the one you mentioned just now—did Jessica ride in that class, too?"

"You mean the one that got Payton's dad to buy her the saddle?" the younger girl asked. "That wasn't a jumper class, it was an eq class."

"A what class?" George asked.

"Eq—that's short for equitation," Rachel explained. "That's where the rider is judged instead of the horse. You know—for having the proper riding position and stuff."

"Okay," I said. "But was Jessica in it too?"

"Jessica doesn't do eq," Rachel said. "She only rides jumpers."

"And hunters, sometimes," the other girl put in. "At least she used to, before she sold her pony."

My head was spinning with all the horse show jargon. But the one fact I needed seemed clear enough regardless of the details. "So Payton didn't beat Jessica out for some big prize in that particular class?"

"Not *that* one." The younger girl giggled. "Just, like, every *other* class Jessica's ever been in."

So the saddle probably wasn't some kind of symbol of a particularly heinous defeat. That didn't necessarily mean Jessica couldn't still be the culprit. But I didn't want to jump to conclusions.

"Anyone else you can think of who might have it out for Payton?" I asked, waiting for Rachel to mention Lenny Hood. After all, she was one of the ones who'd told us about his history with Payton.

Instead it was the younger girl who spoke up. "Um, maybe," she said hesitantly. She paused, shooting a look at Rachel. "What about Cal?"

At that moment Dana burst into the room like a small tornado. "This is the absolute last straw!" she exclaimed breathlessly. "I'm serious. Payton has to stop messing up my life, or I won't be around to live it! Then where will you all be? Who will be there to fix all your disasters and help pick up the pieces, huh? I ask you!" She glared at the two girls, who didn't answer. In fact, both of them were inching backward toward the door.

"Did you find Payton?" I asked, stepping forward. "What did she say about—"

"No, I didn't find Payton!" the trainer cut me off irritably. "You'd think at a small-town show like this, she wouldn't be so hard to track down. Just one more way she's making my life difficult."

She pushed past Bess and snatched the ruined saddle off the rack. Then she stomped toward the door.

"Wait!" I said. "I need to ask you—"

"Sorry," she cut me off again. "I need to find Payton. Like, seriously, *now*."

"Wow," Rachel said once the trainer was gone. "She seemed really mad."

"Yeah." The younger girl grabbed Rachel's arm to

check her watch. "We better go start tacking up, or she'll be mad at us next."

The two of them rushed out of the room without another word. "Leave it to Nancy," George said.

"Leave it to Nancy what?" I asked, distracted by my thoughts.

George smirked. "To show up at an innocent, fun-filled day at the horse show, and have everything go down the drain."

Bess rolled her eyes. "You're blaming Nancy just because a mystery happened to show up where she happened to be?" she said. "That makes about as much sense as Dana blaming Payton because someone vandalized her saddle."

"Right." I was kind of disturbed by the trainer's reaction myself. "It's like Dana can't wait to criticize everything Payton does."

"Think she should be a suspect?" George asked.

"You never know," I said. "But there are a few better ones I want to check out first. Like Jessica Watts, and Lenny Hood, and maybe this Cal that girl just mentioned, whoever that might be."

Bess nodded. "And what about the animal rights group from the parking lot? They're the ones who tossed that tomato."

"True, though I haven't seen any sign that any of them has actually been inside the show grounds, which would make it hard for them to slash the saddle." I paused. "Besides, I can't imagine why they'd be targeting Payton in particular."

"Maybe because she wins a lot?" George suggested. "They might figure it'll make more of a splash for their cause or whatever."

"I don't know. Sounds a little far-fetched. Still, you're right—let's not cross anyone off the list just yet." Spotting Midnight's groom hurrying past outside, I stepped into the aisle. "Hey, Mickey!" I called.

The groom stopped and glanced at me. "Yes?" he said politely, no hint of recognition on his weathered face. "Can I help you?"

"I'm Payton's friend," I prompted him. "Nancy. We met yesterday."

"Oh." Mickey didn't seem interested. But that didn't matter—I wasn't looking for small talk. Just information.

"You've probably seen the animal rights people protesting outside, right?" I said. "I was wondering if you've noticed them at any other shows in the past couple of months. Especially the recent one where Midnight got drug tested?"

For the first time, the groom showed a glimmer of emotion. Namely, confusion. "I don't know. I don't usually leave the grounds much during a show." He shrugged. "Didn't hear anything about any protesters the past few shows, though."

"Did you hear about the ones at *this* show?" George asked.

"Yeah." The groom shot her a look. "I heard. Had to clean their mess off Midnight's coat yesterday, didn't I?"

"Okay, one more question," I said. "Do you know of anyone around here named Cal?"

"Cal?" Mickey blinked. "The only Cal I know of is Cal Kidd. He's a jumper rider—and he's the one who sold Midnight to Payton."

CHAPTER SEVEN

Research and Gossip

BEFORE I COULD QUESTION MICKEY FURther, his cell phone buzzed. "Excuse me," he said after glancing at the screen. "I have to go."

He hurried off. "He's not exactly Mr. Chatty, is he?" Bess said.

"It's okay. At least now we have a name." I glanced at George. "Feel like looking up Cal Kidd on your smartphone?"

"On it." George pulled out her fancy phone, a gift from her parents for her last birthday. Her fingers flew over the keypad.

"So this Cal is Midnight's former owner," Bess mused, leaning against the door frame of the tack room as we waited. "If he sold the horse to Payton, why would he be mad at her now? I don't get it."

"I don't either," I said. "Maybe he thinks she cheated him on the price somehow? Although that wouldn't make much sense either, since her parents would have been the ones actually paying, right?"

"Got it," George spoke up. "There are quite a few articles about Cal Kidd on the web." She held the phone's tiny screen closer to her face, scanning whatever was on there. "Whoa. Looks like he's had some gambling problems. Got in a bunch of debt, even went to prison for a bit. Was out of the whole horse show scene for a couple of years and is just now getting back into it."

"Really?" That sounded interesting. I leaned closer. "Anything about Midnight on there?"

"Hold on, I'm reading. . . ." George went silent.

Bess glanced down the aisle. "Someone's coming," she said. "Maybe we should find a more private spot to talk about this."

I nodded, following her gaze. A gaggle of tweens in riding clothes were coming our way, chattering excitedly at one another.

"Let's go," I said, grabbing George's elbow and steering her down the aisle in the opposite direction. She didn't say a word—just kept reading, occasionally hitting a key with her thumb.

The show grounds were getting busy by now, and it wasn't easy to find a spot where we wouldn't be overheard. Finally we happened upon a small courtyard behind the show office. Nobody was out there, and it was hidden from the main path by a line of shrubs and a large Dumpster.

"Yuck, not exactly my favorite," Bess said, glancing at the flies buzzing around the Dumpster.

"Never mind, we won't be here long." I turned to George. "What've you got?"

George looked up from her phone. "Okay, here's the gist of this Cal Kidd guy's history." She started pacing back and forth like an overcaffeinated university lecturer. "He was some big-time jumper rider for years—started winning big classes when he was almost as young as Payton. Everyone thought he was destined for the Olympic show-jumping team."

"Sounds familiar," Bess put in.

"Yeah. He had lots of sponsors buying him horses and riders wanting him to be their trainer. Only then, like I said, he got mixed up in gambling. Ended up in serious debt, lost all his supporters and clients, and had to sell off his horses."

"Including Midnight?" Bess asked.

"Yeah. That's the weird thing, though." George stopped pacing and glanced down at the phone in her hand. "It sounds like Midnight wasn't even one of his better horses. In fact, it sounds like he didn't have much success with him at all, even though he won everything there was to win on every other horse he rode." She shrugged. "Midnight didn't start winning anything important until after Payton bought him."

"Interesting." I stared at the brick wall of the office building, trying to fit this into what we knew about the case so far. "Could Cal be trying to get Midnight back now that the horse is a superstar—a potential Olympic horse?"

"Could be," George agreed. "That would be a good way to jump-start his return to the sport." She grinned. "Did you see what I did there? *Jump*-start?"

"Yeah, you're a comic genius," Bess said dryly. She turned to me. "But would he really want Midnight back? George just said Cal didn't have much luck with him the first time. Maybe they didn't get along."

"Maybe. I don't know. But it's worth checking out." I chewed on my lower lip, trying to figure out how to proceed. "I should've asked Mickey if Cal is at this show."

"One way to find out." Bess pointed at the building in front of us. "Let's go ask at the office."

Within minutes, we had the information we needed. The pleasant woman manning the show secretary's desk told us that Cal Kidd had reserved a block of three stalls at the show. She even pointed us in the right direction.

My friends and I headed that way. "So what are you going to say to Cal Kidd?" Bess asked me.

"I'm not sure yet," I said. "I guess I'll just mention Midnight and then—hold on, is that my phone?"

I dug my cell phone out of my pocket. A text had just arrived from Ned:

FOUND P. SHE & D ARE TALKING PRIVATELY IN THE TACK RM.

George peered at the screen. "Yikes," she said. "I'm surprised we can't hear Dana yelling from here."

I grimaced, then sent a quick response:

KEEP US POSTED. B, G, & I ARE CHECKING OUT A LEAD.

"I wonder how Payton is taking the news about Midnight's drug-test results," Bess said. "She seemed pretty broken up by that drugging accusation yesterday—this is much worse."

"Yeah." I squinted at the number on the barn we were approaching. "Look, I think we're almost to Cal Kidd's stalls."

It took another few minutes of wandering around and asking people for help before we found our way to the very back of the barn, where Cal Kidd's three stalls were tucked into a corner. Unlike Dana's section in her barn, which was spotless and fully decked out in her barn colors, Cal's area here seemed a bit shabby and bare. However, the horses looking out of the three stalls appeared healthy and well groomed.

"Hello?" I called as Bess patted a curious chestnut mare. "Mr. Kidd?"

There was no response. A woman sweeping the aisle in front of the next block of stalls looked our way. "You looking for Cal?" she called in a friendly tone. "He's not here."

I stepped closer. "Do you know when he'll be back?"

"Not sure. Haven't seen him all day, actually," the woman said. "I talked to him a bit yesterday, and I don't think he has any classes today, so I guess he might not be back until feeding time tonight. Want me to let him know you were looking for him if I see him then?"

I was disappointed, but tried not to let it show. "Um, that's okay. We'll just check back later. Thanks."

Returning to my friends, I told them what the woman had said. "Guess there's no point hanging around here, then." Bess gave the chestnut one last pat, then stepped back. "Maybe we should head back and see what's going on with Payton."

"Hey, did you guys see this?" George was peering up at a cork bulletin board hanging between two of the stalls. It was the only bit of decoration in Cal's area, containing several ribbons and photos, though I'd barely glanced at it before. "This must be Cal Kidd. Look familiar?"

I stepped closer. "Yeah," I said. "That looks like the same guy we saw yesterday. The one who seemed so angry when Payton beat him in that first class we watched."

George nodded. "I think you guys are right. The photos on my phone were so small that I didn't recognize him before."

"So that's interesting," Bess said. "First Payton turns Cal's old horse into a big success, then she starts beating him during his big comeback."

"That can't be easy to take, especially since she's, like, half his age," George added. "Think it's enough of a motive to mess with her?"

"Maybe." I stared at the photo for a moment, then turned away. "Come on, let's go find Ned."

As we walked out of the barn, George started fiddling with her cell phone again. "What are you doing?" Bess asked.

"Looking up our other suspects," George replied. "Lenny Hood and Jessica Watts."

"Finding anything interesting?" I asked.

"Not yet—just regular stuff about their show results or whatever." George tapped a few more keys. "I'll let you know."

She was still searching when we neared the building where Dana's block of stalls was located. Just outside, half a dozen teenage riders were gathered by the benches outside the barn entrance. As we neared them, I was pretty sure I heard Payton's name.

"Hold up," I whispered, stopping my friends.

George looked up from her phone screen. "Huh?"

I shushed her, trying to hear what the teens were saying. A pretty brunette was talking. ". . . and if she gets suspended, there's no way they'll even consider giving her a chance at the team this year."

Another girl pursed her lips. "I bet she did it. She's so intense—like she'd do anything to win."

"Yeah," a third rider put in. "Plus, if you ask me, there's no way someone her age could win all those big jumper classes without a little, you know, extra help." She smirked as several of the others giggled.

"Come on, you guys," a petite blond girl spoke up. "I think Payton's really sweet, and she seems super honest, too. Maybe it wasn't her fault."

That was all I needed to hear. I strode forward to confront them. "Are you guys talking about Payton Evans?" I asked.

The girls all looked startled. One of them, a tall redhead with freckles all over her face, met my eye.

"Who wants to know?" she asked.

"I do," I responded evenly. "I'm a friend of Payton's. If there's something going on, I'd like to know about it."

The redhead considered that for a moment, then glanced at the others. "Whatever," she said at last.

"Everyone is going to know soon anyway. Payton's Grand Prix horse just flunked a drug test."

"Yeah," the brunette put in, her eyes flashing with excitement at the gossip. "And Payton's supposed to ride him tomorrow night!"

"If Midnight ends up on the suspended list, that'll be the end of that," another girl said.

"But I heard the test result was actually sort of inconclusive or whatever," the blonde said. "The committee gets to decide whether they're going to suspend or just give a warning."

"Do you think they'll decide before tomorrow?" George asked. "That's when the Grand Prix is, right? The one the Olympic guy is coming to watch?"

"Yeah," the redhead said. "And I bet they'll decide before then. Otherwise it'll look bad if the news gets out."

"And it will." The brunette giggled. "I bet the entire show grounds knows by the end of today!"

"You know that's got to be killing Dana," one of the others put in. "I'd pay to see that freak-out!"

The girls already seemed to have forgotten that my friends and I were there. Or maybe they were just too caught up in their gossip to care. I was about to move on when something occurred to me. The last I'd heard, even Payton hadn't found out about the test results yet. I supposed that was what she and Dana were discussing when Ned texted me, but that was only about twenty minutes ago. How had the gossip spread so fast?

I cleared my throat to remind the girls I was still there. "Where did you first hear about this?" I asked, focusing on the redhead, who seemed to be the ring-leader.

"News travels fast around here," she said breezily.

Not good enough. "No, seriously," I pressed her. "Who told you about the drug-test results?"

The girl seemed taken aback that I was pressing the point. For the first time her bravado wavered, and she shot a quick, uncertain look at the pretty brunette. Aha.

"Well?" I asked, turning my attention to the bru-nette. "How'd you hear? Did someone tell you, or were you skulking around in the barns eavesdropping on people?"

The brunette frowned. "I wasn't eavesdropping," she said, sounding insulted. "Someone told me, okay?"

"Okay. So who was it?"

She looked stubborn. "Who are you, anyway?" she asked, crossing her arms over her chest. "I've never seen you guys at the shows before."

"She told you, we're friends of Payton's," George said. "Now spill it. Who told you?"

"Just tell them already, Val." The redhead sounded bored now. "It's not like Jessica was even being sneaky about it. I'm sure she's told lots of people already."

"Jessica?" I said quickly. "Do you mean Jessica Watts?"

"Yeah." The brunette sounded surly. "Whatever, it might've been her. But you didn't hear that from me, okay?"

I traded a quick look with Bess and George. How in the world had Jessica found out about the test result so quickly? It wasn't as if she and Payton were friends—far from it. Then again, if she was the one who'd slipped something to the horse, she might have some kind of insider knowledge. . . .

I opened my mouth to ask how long ago Jessica had started spreading the news. Before I could get a word out, a loud shout cut me off:

"Look out—loose horses!"

CHAPTER EIGHT

Fast and Loose

MORE VOICES CAME FROM VARIOUS DIREC-
tions, picking up the shout: *"Loose horses! Loose horses!"*

"Oh my gosh," one of the teen girls said. "I hope
my pony didn't duck out under his stall guard again!"

She and the other girls rushed off around the corner of the barn. My friends and I followed, swept up by
the general excitement.

"Uh-oh," George said as we rounded the corner
and skidded to a stop.

Three horses were running around wildly in the
grassy area between barns. Two of them were big

bays, and the third was a rangy liver chestnut.

"That's not Midnight, is it?" Bess said, pointing at one of the bays.

George gasped. "It *does* look like him! And check it out, there's Dana trying to grab him."

I saw that George was right. Payton's trainer was among those trying to catch the loose horses. She was moving slowly toward the excited bay, her arms out as she spoke soothingly to him.

"Hold up. Actually, I don't think it's Midnight." I peered at the horse. It was hard to get a good look, since he was currently dodging back and forth trying to avoid Dana. But then he lifted his head so I had a clear view of his face. "Nope, it's not him," I said with relief. "See? That horse has a white star on his face, and Midnight doesn't."

"Oh, you're right," Bess said. "Look, I think Dana's got him."

We watched as several people, including some of the teenage girls we'd just been talking to, helped catch the other two horses. Soon all three escapees were heading back into the barn.

"Whew, that was kind of crazy," George said. "The action never stops around here!"

Bess laughed, but I just rubbed my chin. "Yeah," I agreed. "It's kind of suspicious, isn't it?"

George looked surprised. "What do you mean? Do you think someone let the horses out on purpose? Why?"

"Yeah," Bess put in. "Especially since none of them belonged to Payton."

"I know. But doesn't it seem awfully coincidental that one of them was a big bay gelding from Dana's barn? One that looks a lot like Midnight?" I shrugged. "I mean, we all mistook him for Midnight for a second there. Maybe someone else did too."

"Oh!" Bess's eyes widened. "I didn't think of that. So you think this really could be connected to the case?"

"I don't know. But we can't rule it out. Let's go find Payton. I think we need to talk to her about all this."

We headed into the barn. A couple of grooms and a middle-aged woman were fussing over the recently recaptured bay gelding, who was now standing quietly cross-tied in the aisle.

"Excuse me, do you know where Dana went?" I asked one of the grooms.

"I'm not sure." The groom seemed distracted as he ran a rag down the horse's legs. "Tack room, maybe? She was talking to Payton in there when the horses got loose."

"Thanks." I led the way down the aisle.

As my friends and I neared the tack room, we could hear the sound of a raised voice. "Uh-oh," Bess whispered. "Sounds like Dana's not happy."

"Sounds like Payton's not either," I said as another angry voice joined in.

I wasn't sure we should be listening to their argument. But it wasn't as if they were making any attempt to be quiet—half the barn could probably hear them. My friends and I took a few steps closer, stopping just short of the doorway.

". . . and it's like you don't even care about your own reputation anymore, let alone mine!" Dana was yelling.

"That's not fair!" Payton exclaimed, sounding upset. "If it was up to me, I wouldn't even be at this show!"

"Huh?" George murmured, raising an eyebrow at Bess and me.

"Shh," I hushed her, leaning closer to the door.

"Look, I know you're upset about missing your friend's party or whatever—," Dana began.

"It's my cousin," Payton snapped, cutting her off. "My favorite cousin, who's been like an older sister to me my whole life. And it's not just some party—it's her *wedding*!"

"Okay, whatever, I'm sorry," Dana said. "But in this industry, you need to be willing to make sacrifices. And it's not every day that the chef d'équipe wants to show up and watch you ride. . . ."

Unfortunately, she lowered her voice just enough so it was impossible to make out whatever she said next. I backed up a few yards, and my friends followed.

"This adds a new wrinkle," I said quietly. "It sounds like Payton wanted to skip this show to go to her cousin's wedding."

"I wonder if that's the family obligation that's keeping her parents away until tomorrow night," Bess said.

"Probably," I agreed, remembering Payton's comment the day before. "In any case, Dana must've insisted she skip the wedding so she could ride in front of the Olympics guy."

"Maybe Payton's parents, too," George said. "It sounds like they're pretty competitive and ambitious."

"Yeah. Even if it wasn't their idea, they must've agreed with Dana. Because if they thought Payton should go to the wedding instead, they could've overruled her." I shook my head. "You know, I'm starting to feel really sorry for Payton. On the one hand, she's living out her dream—riding at these big shows, super successful, aimed for Olympic glory."

Bess nodded, clearly seeing where I was going with my thought. "But there's a dark side too," she said. "Her life isn't really her own. She has to make sacrifices to be the best." She sighed. "It's just too bad Dana seems to be so, you know, *mean* about it."

"Yeah." George glanced in the direction of the tack

room. "She really doesn't sound too sympathetic, does she?"

Her comment made another thought pop into my head. It was one that had been dancing around at the edges of my thoughts all day.

"You're right," I said slowly. "If Dana's the one who forced Payton to come to this show, could that be a clue in itself?"

"What do you mean?" Bess asked. "Do you think Dana should be a suspect?"

"I'm not sure," I said. "I mean, this isn't the first time we've witnessed her being kind of hard on Payton. But if she's the culprit, what's her motive?"

"Good question." George pursed her lips thoughtfully. "She's Payton's trainer. So if Payton looks good, she looks good, right? Why would she want to mess that up?"

"And would she really slash up that saddle?" Bess wondered. "I mean, she seems kind of hot-tempered, but not *crazy*."

"Yeah, I can't quite picture her going at the saddle

with a knife either," I admitted. "Still, we'd better put her on the list. Just in case." Something else occurred to me. "And actually, even if she's not the best suspect for some of the stuff that's happened, there's one thing that fits perfectly. She's the one in charge of Midnight's care, right? Including everything he eats. So she was in the best position to toss some chocolate or whatever into his bucket to make him flunk that test, right?"

"I guess so." Bess looked uncertain. "But if that's true, wouldn't she get in trouble too?"

"I don't know." I realized I still wasn't clear on how the whole suspension system worked. "Let's see if we can find someone to ask."

George glanced toward the tack room. "Good idea. We probably shouldn't be here when they come out."

I had to agree with that. If Dana might be our culprit, it probably wasn't a good thing for her to catch us eavesdropping.

My friends and I tiptoed away around the corner, then started looking around for someone to ask about the drug rules. The first familiar face we saw belonged to Mickey. He was outside Midnight's stall, stuffing hay into a hay net. The big bay gelding was watching the man's work with interest.

"Hi." I walked over and gave Midnight a rub on the nose, then smiled at the groom. "Do you have a second?"

This time I was pretty sure he recognized me, though he seemed less than thrilled to see me. "Uh, I guess," he mumbled without enthusiasm.

"We were just talking about Midnight's drug results, and we realized we don't understand how the system works," I said. "Who gets suspended when something like that happens?"

"The horse does, of course. Plus whoever signs on the entry form as that horse's primary caretaker," Mickey replied, yanking the cords to tie the hay net shut. "Normally that's the trainer, unless the owner signs as trainer for some reason."

"Oh." I shot a look at my friends. What Mickey was saying seemed to rule out our latest theory, since Dana would be the one who got suspended rather than Payton.

Mickey hung the hay net just outside the stall door, patting Midnight as the big bay horse eagerly yanked a few strands out and chewed. "Wouldn't be the worst thing for this guy to get suspended," the groom murmured, running one calloused hand up and down the gelding's neck. His voice was so low that I wasn't sure he'd meant to be overheard.

"What was that?" I asked. "Did you say it would be *good* for Midnight to get suspended?"

"'Course not," he said gruffly. "It's just that Midnight could use a break, that's all. He's been campaigned pretty hard this year. Too many weeks standing in a tiny stall, riding in trailers . . . Ah, never mind. Stupid thought."

"No, I understand." Bess shot the man her most winning and sympathetic smile. "You're just worried about Midnight. I think that's sweet."

Mickey merely grunted in response. But his expression lightened a little bit. Bess has that effect on people. I don't know how she does it.

"Yeah, you must be really worried about what

happened," I said, trying to sound casual. A lot of people are more likely to talk if they don't realize they're being interrogated. I had a feeling Mickey was one of those people. "Especially since someone obviously tried to hurt Midnight by dosing him with theobromine." I reached out to stroke the gelding's velvety nose. "That can't be good for him, right?"

"Not likely to hurt him," Mickey responded. "Especially not in such a small amount."

"Oh. That's good," I said. "Still, who would want to give him something they knew would test? And how would they even do it?" I eyed the hay net as Midnight took another bite. "Do you think someone sneaked in and slipped something into his food?"

"Not likely." Mickey sounded certain. "We've got a foolproof system here."

"You do? What is it?"

The groom shrugged. "Really want to know? I'll show you." He headed off down the aisle without another word.

Trading a look with my friends, I shrugged and

then followed. Soon we were all crowding into a stall at the end of the row. Like the tack stall, it wasn't set up for horses. Instead it contained at least a dozen large feed sacks, piles of empty buckets, a folding table with a bunch of small plastic bags on it, and a bunch of other stuff I didn't take in right away. Tacked to one wall was a poster-board list of horses' names written in different colors. Beside each name was some additional writing in black ink, though it was too small to read from where I was standing.

"Feed room," Mickey said, and I hid a smile. I knew where we were.

"So all the horses' grain comes from here?" George asked, peering into a large bag labeled as alfalfa pellets.

"Uh-huh." Mickey pointed to a neat row of buckets along one wall. "One color for each horse. Feed gets measured out there." Next he indicated the plastic bags on the table. "Supplements there."

"Supplements?" I echoed.

"Vitamins. Joint aids. Stuff like that," Mickey said. "When it's time to feed, grab the bag and dump it in the matching bucket. No way to mix things up."

Bess stepped closer to the poster and peered up at the list of names. "Midnight's color is purple," she said. She moved over to the line of buckets. "Hey, wait a minute. It looks like someone already added some supplements to this purple bucket."

"Can't be." George picked up a plastic bag filled with powder. A purple sticker was on it. "His bag's right here."

Mickey frowned. "What are you talking about?" He glanced at the bag in George's hand, then stepped over and peered into the purple bucket. His face went pale, and he grabbed the bucket with one hand, reaching into it with the other. "There *is* some kind of powder in here!" he exclaimed. Lifting his fingers to his nose, he gave them a sniff. "Smells like bute. But that can't be! Midnight isn't supposed to get that!"

CHAPTER NINE

Mixed Messages

"BUTE? WHAT'S THAT?" GEORGE ASKED.

Mickey didn't answer. He was already sprinting toward the door, calling out for the other grooms. "Nobody feed anything!" he shouted. "I've got to tell Dana about this. We'll have to figure out if any of the other feed was tampered with."

A couple of the other grooms rushed in. They seemed surprised to see us in there.

"What's going on?" asked Jen.

"We're not sure," I told her. "Um, Mickey just noticed there was some extra stuff in one of the buckets."

"Yeah, he called it bute," George added. "What is that?"

"It's a medication," Jen replied. "It's very common—sort of like aspirin for horses. Some of ours get it after a tough day of showing. Which bucket was it in?"

"Midnight's," Bess replied.

"What?" Jen exclaimed. "But that's not right—Midnight isn't allowed to have bute today!"

"Why not?" I asked. "I thought you said it was common."

The groom looked distraught. "It is, but you're not allowed to give it at the same time as certain other drugs," she explained. "And Midnight is scheduled to get one of those other drugs tonight. If he ended up with both in his system and then got tested . . ."

She let her voice trail off. I could guess what she was thinking. Midnight was in enough trouble with the drug testers already, without another positive result to add to the mess.

"Anyway," Jen went on after a moment, "I know there was nothing extra in that bucket an hour ago—

I mixed all of this afternoon's feed myself!"

She and the other groom started checking all the buckets. My friends and I took the opportunity to slip out of the feed room.

"So what do you think?" George asked as we wandered down the aisle. "Does this make Mickey a suspect?"

"Maybe," I said. "It sounds like he wouldn't mind one bit if Midnight got a vacation. And a drug suspension would be a sure way to do it."

Bess nodded. "Especially since he was so quick to tell us that the theo-whatever stuff the test found wouldn't hurt Midnight any. That makes it a likely choice for someone who's worried about the horse's welfare, right?"

"Good point." I couldn't help feeling dubious. "But if he's the culprit, why would he just blurt all that info out to us? I mean, he pretty much handed us his motive on a silver platter."

"Guilty conscience?" George suggested.

We'd reached the barn exit by then. Bess paused in

the doorway, squinting against the sunlight streaming in from outside. "No, maybe Nancy's right," she said. "Mickey seemed genuinely surprised and upset when he saw that powder in Midnight's bucket just now. Either he's a really good actor . . ."

"Or he's not the one who put it there," I finished for her. "Besides, I just thought of something else. Mickey said it's the *trainer* who gets suspended when a horse fails a drug test. Not the owner or rider. So Dana would be the one going down. Would Mickey really want to get his boss suspended from showing? Seems like that could be bad for his own income."

"I don't know," George said. "But I just remembered something else. Mickey was hanging around when Payton took Midnight out to graze yesterday. But then when we came back after the tomato incident, he was nowhere in sight. Remember? Payton handed Midnight off to another groom."

"So what?" Bess said.

"So what if Mickey was out in the parking lot convincing those PAN loonies to tomato-bomb a certain big bay horse?" George said. "It could've all been part of his plan to scare Payton into quitting so Midnight would get a chance to go lounge in a field or whatever."

I sighed. "The more we talk about Mickey as a suspect, the more far-fetched it seems," I said. "I mean, I could maybe see him slipping something into Midnight's feed or whatever, thinking he's doing the horse a favor. But would he really follow Payton around leaving nasty notes, or convince someone to toss tomatoes, or slash up a saddle, or let a bunch of other horses loose?"

"Who knows?" George shrugged. "We don't know the guy. Maybe he's a secret psycho."

I didn't respond. I'd just noticed someone hurrying past outside. "Hey," I said, lowering my voice. "Isn't that Jessica Watts?"

"Where?" George turned to look. "Yeah, that's her. What's she doing hanging around this barn?"

"Good question." I watched as Jessica disappeared around the corner. "I mean, it's a public place, so it's probably a coincidence. Maybe her horses are in this barn too. Maybe she has friends in this barn. Maybe she's looking for the bathroom."

"Or maybe she's sneaking out after tampering with Midnight's feed bucket," George said. "Let's follow her and see where she goes."

I didn't have any better plan to suggest, so I nodded. "Stay back so she doesn't see us," I warned as we hurried off in the direction the girl had gone.

George tossed me an amused look. "What, do you think this is our first stakeout?" she joked.

"Shh!" Bess warned as we rounded the corner. "There she is."

We tailed Jessica halfway across the show grounds. She didn't seem to be in any hurry. Every so often she would wave to someone passing by or even pause to say hello. Finally she entered a snack bar.

"Looks like she's just looking for something to eat," Bess said.

"Maybe not." George had darted forward to peer inside through a window. "Look who she's talking to now!"

Bess and I joined her at the window. "Oh!" Bess exclaimed softly. "It's that nasty trainer—what's his name again?"

"Lenny Hood." I gripped the edge of the window as I stared inside. Payton and Lenny Hood were standing at the back of the small restaurant, heads bent together as they talked. I couldn't see Jessica's face, but Lenny's expression was focused and intense.

"I wish we could hear what they're saying," Bess murmured.

"Me too," I said. "What if they're in cahoots, working together to frame Payton for that drug violation?"

"Exactly what I was thinking," George said. "With Payton out of the picture, Jessica would have a better shot at some of those ribbons. And the prize money that goes with them."

"Lenny Hood's students, too," Bess agreed. "Think we can get any closer?"

"Not without them seeing us," I said. "Let's just wait and see what they do next."

We didn't have long to wait. Within minutes,

Jessica and Lenny were leaving the snack bar. My friends and I stayed hidden around the corner, though it probably wasn't necessary, since neither of our culprits so much as glanced our way before hurrying off in opposite directions.

"Now what?" Bess asked. "Should we split up and follow them?"

I didn't answer for a second. I'd just spotted another familiar face wandering into view across the way. "Look," I said. "Isn't that Cal Kidd?"

Bess gasped. "What's he doing here? I thought he wasn't at the show today."

"That's what his neighbor told me," I said. "Looks like she was wrong."

"So what do you want to do?" George glanced after Lenny, who was almost out of sight already. "If we don't hurry, we'll lose track of all of them."

"I'll follow Cal," I decided quickly. "You guys take the other two, okay?"

I rushed off, leaving it to them to work out the details. Cal was strolling along with his hands in his pockets, not seeming in any particular hurry. It was easy to keep him in sight as he wandered along the paths, pausing once to watch a pony trotting around in one of the schooling rings and again to pat a free-ranging dog.

Finally I realized he was heading toward the big old-fashioned wooden barn, where his show stalls were located. I waited until he'd disappeared inside, then cautiously entered myself. It was busier in there than it had been earlier in the day, and I had no trouble making my way to the back section without Cal noticing me.

I hid in the hayloft with a view of Cal's area and waited to see what he did next. For a while, that wasn't much. He puttered around for a good twenty minutes—first checking on each of his horses, then sweeping the aisle by his stalls. Finally he grabbed a magazine with a horse on the cover, sat down on a tack trunk, and started flipping through the pages.

Sneaking a peek at my watch, I wondered what to do. By the looks of things, I could stand here all day and see nothing important. Why waste time when every second counted? Still, Cal was on the suspect list. I had to figure out whether he needed to stay there.

That meant it was time to stop spying and take some action. I climbed down from my hiding place and walked right over to Cal.

"Hello," I said. "You're Cal Kidd, right?"

He glanced up from his magazine. "That's me. And you are?"

"My name's Nancy," I said. "I'm, uh, a journalism student. I'm here interviewing people at this horse show as part of a class project."

"Cool." Cal's smile was polite but a little distant. "So lay it on me. What do you want to know?"

I scanned my mind for a good opening question that wouldn't make him suspicious. "Um, you're a jumper rider, right? What made you get into that?"

"It's kind of a family thing." Cal tossed aside the magazine and stood, stepping over to pat the nearest of his horses. He had only a couple of inches on me, though he was so lean that he seemed taller. "My mom rode when my sister and I were kids, and we just kind of followed along in her footsteps. Or boot steps. Whatever." He grinned.

I had to admit he was kind of charming. No wonder he'd had so many clients and admirers before his fall from grace. Then again, I'd learned long ago that appearances could be deceiving. Some of the worst criminals I'd nabbed—or that Dad had helped convict—could seem like the most agreeable people in the world.

"Okay," I said. "What's your favorite thing about the sport?"

"The horses, of course. Though the speed and thrill aren't bad, either." Cal glanced at me. "Hey, don't you need to, like, write this down or record it or something? I'm feeding you pearls of wisdom here!" His grin faded slightly as he studied my face. "Wait a minute, you look kind of familiar—didn't I see you hanging around with Payton Evans yesterday?"

Oops. I hadn't realized he'd even seen us by the ring after Payton's round. "Um, yeah," I said. "I was interviewing her, too."

"Hmm." Suddenly Cal looked a lot less friendly.

"Well, here's some more info for your class project. The big-time show-jumping world is a tough business, not a game of My Little Pony, okay?"

"I'm not sure what you mean." I backed away, feeling nervous all of a sudden.

His eyes narrowed. "I mean it's no place for little girls," he growled. "You can tell your friend Payton Evans that the next time you interview her. Now if you'll excuse me, I have business to attend to."

He stalked off, glowering, and disappeared around the corner. I collapsed against the wall, my heart pounding. I knew I should probably follow him to see where he was going. But after the threat he'd just made, I was none too eager to face him again.

"If it *was* a threat," I murmured to myself, still not quite sure what had just happened. Either way, his reaction was weird enough to keep his name on the suspect list for sure.

"Here she comes," George said.

Following her gaze, I saw Bess jogging toward us.

We were behind the show office again. I'd texted both my friends after leaving Cal's barn, telling them to meet me there whenever they were finished.

"I hope you guys found out something interesting." Bess was huffing and puffing as she reached us. "Because my detective work was a total bust."

"Really? What happened?" I asked.

Bess leaned against the wall to catch her breath. "Nothing, pretty much," she said. "Lenny went back to his barn and talked on his cell phone for a while. Not about anything interesting, as far as I could hear. Then he went over to one of the rings to watch some of his students ride. He was still there when I left."

"Okay." I turned to George. She'd arrived just moments before Bess, so we hadn't had a chance to compare notes yet. "What about you?" I asked.

"I followed Jessica back to her barn," George said. "She sat down on a tack trunk and started texting, so I got bored and took a look around."

Bess snorted. "Some detective you are, Ms. Short Attention Span."

George ignored her. "Anyway, I ended up chatting with Jessica's trainer. And guess what I found out?"

"What?" I asked.

"It turns out Jessica might be a jerk, but she's not our culprit." George looked pleased with herself. "Because she wasn't even *at* the show where Midnight got tested."

"Are you sure?" I asked.

"Positive. The trainer lady knew exactly which show I was talking about. I guess she's friends with Dana—she'd just heard the gossip and seemed pretty bummed out that Midnight might get suspended. She said the rest of the barn was at the show in question, but Jessica had the flu or something that week."

"Interesting." I twirled a lock of hair around my finger as I tried to fit this piece into the puzzle.

Bess was frowning. "So this means Jessica couldn't be our culprit, right?" she said. "She wasn't around to slip something into Midnight's food at that show."

"Right," I said. "Unless she really is in cahoots with Lenny Hood, of course."

"Oh, right." George's face fell. "I forgot about that."

"Actually, with all the weird stuff that's happening, it's seeming more and more likely that there could be more than one culprit at work," I said. "That would certainly make it easier to make all the pieces fit."

"Okay," Bess said. "So what do we do now?"

"I'm not sure." I glanced at the sky, which was showing streaks of red. "It's getting late, and the show will be winding down for the night pretty soon. Maybe we should find Payton and see what she wants to do."

My phone buzzed before my friends could respond. It was a text from Ned, asking where we were. Oops. In all the excitement, I'd forgotten to update him in a while.

I let him know where we were, and he was there within minutes. "What have you been up to all day?" Bess asked him. "Planning some romantic getaway for your anniversary?"

"Actually, yes." Ned grinned and winked, then turned to take my hand. "I'm officially sweeping you away with me."

"Huh?" I said.

"Since we had to cancel our picnic, I want to make it up to you," Ned said. "I'm taking you out to dinner. What do you say?"

"Picnic? What picnic?" Bess asked.

Ned ignored her. "So how's Italian sound?" he asked, squeezing my hand.

My stomach grumbled, and I realized I'd forgotten to eat lunch. "It sounds fantastic." I glanced at my friends. "Can you guys finish up here without me? We should probably check in with Payton, and—"

"Go." Bess gave me a little shove. "Have a nice time." She pulled me back toward her, gave a sniff, and wrinkled her nose. "But for Pete's sake, stop off at home and take a shower first. You smell like a horse!"

"This is nice," I said, reaching for my water glass. The ice cubes clinked against the crystal as I took a sip. I glanced around. We were seated in the crowded dining room of the most popular Italian restaurant in River

Heights. "I can't believe you actually got us a table here on a Friday night."

Across from me, Ned looked happy and handsome as he lifted his own water glass in a toast. "Only the best for you," he said with a wink. Then he chuckled. "But seriously, it's only because my mom plays tennis with the owner. Don't tell Bess that, though."

"Your secret's safe with me." My smile faded as I returned my attention to my pasta. It was delicious, even though I could barely remember ordering it. In fact, I'd spent most of the two-plus hours since leaving the show grounds only half-focused on what I was doing. The rest of my mind kept returning to the case. The Grand Prix was tomorrow night, and I had no idea when the powers that be would make their decision about whether Payton and Midnight could still enter. If I didn't figure something out fast, there was a chance Payton could miss her chance to impress the Olympic chef d'équipe. And I didn't want that to happen if I could help it.

It took me a moment to realize that Ned had said

something. Blinking, I shot him a sheepish smile. "What? Um, sorry. Guess I'm a little distracted."

He looked sympathetic. "I hear you. I'm worried about Payton too."

I reached over and squeezed his hand, grateful as always that he was so understanding about my sleuthing. "Thanks. It's just that we don't have much time, and—"

"I know." Ned speared a meatball with his fork. "I called Mom and Dad to tell them Dana would be dropping Payton off when they finished for the day. They asked how everything went, but I didn't mention that slashed-up saddle. Now I'm wondering it it's a mistake to keep it from them. Whoever did that has some serious anger issues."

"Maybe Payton will tell them when she gets home," I said.

"Maybe." Ned sounded dubious. "But she's the one who didn't even want to tell her parents about that note." He sighed, setting down his fork. "I'm thinking it might be almost time to bring in the police."

I didn't answer. I couldn't really disagree with his point.

"Things just aren't coming together," I mused, staring at my plate. "There are a lot of people on our suspect list, but none of them quite fits all the evidence."

"I know. Like that girl Jessica—she's got a motive, but she wasn't at the show where Midnight got drugged," Ned said. "Plus, could she really sneak into Dana's barn in broad daylight to slash that saddle or tamper with Midnight's feed without anyone seeing her?"

"I'm not sure. We did see her outside right after those horses were let loose. But what about those threatening notes? I'm not even sure she's old enough to drive—how would she follow Payton all the way back to your house?"

"Unless she's teaming up with that other trainer like you said," Ned said.

I nodded. I'd filled Ned in on our latest theories on the ride over. "These big-time trainers all seem to attend most of the same shows, so I'm guessing Lenny was probably at the one in question," I said. "But everyone says he's super successful in the show world. Would he really risk his whole reputation on this kind of garbage, just to take out a teenager?"

Ned shrugged. "Okay, change of pace—how about those animal protester people?"

"You mean PAN?" We'd passed the protesters on our way out of the show, though I'd noticed that Annie Molina wasn't with them. "I don't know. I'm not sure they'd be likely to target any particular person, and so far everything seems to be aimed at Payton."

"Good point." Ned reached for the salt. "They did throw that tomato, though, right?"

"Yeah, but we're wondering if someone put them up to it." That made me realize we'd never followed up on that particular angle. I made a mental note to try to talk to Annie or one of her cohorts the next day.

"Okay," Ned said. "So other than Lenny and Jessica, who else have you got? What about that Cal Kidd guy? Or Dana? Or the groom?"

"All still on the list." I sighed. "It's just that none of

them quite . . . hold on." My phone was buzzing from my purse. Fishing it out, I saw that I'd just received a text. It was from Payton:

NANCY, SORRY 2 BOTHER U—I'M STILL AT THE SHOW, EVERYONE ELSE WENT HOME, & NOW I THINK SOMEONE IS STALKING ME!

CHAPTER TEN

Signing Statement

"CAN'T YOU DRIVE ANY FASTER?" I COM-plained, gripping the armrest of Ned's car.

"Not without breaking the sound barrier." Ned spun the steering wheel, sending his car screeching into the fairgrounds' parking lot. It was a much different sight from the one we'd left a couple of hours earlier. Only a few cars were still parked there, along with several large horse trailers hulking in the pale floodlights positioned here and there throughout the lot.

Ned screeched to a stop near the gate, not bothering to park between the lines. "Let's go," I said, hopping out of the car.

We sprinted in through the gate, the guard barely looking up as we passed. "Where did she say she was?" Ned asked.

"She didn't." I put on a burst of speed. "Let's check Dana's barn. If Payton's not there, I'll text her again."

We burst into the barn. It was dim and quiet in there, the only light coming from a few safety bulbs in the aisle.

"Payton!" Ned hollered. "Where are you? It's Ned and Nancy! Payton!"

I held my breath, listening for a response. "There," I said, spinning and pointing toward the tack stall. "I heard footsteps."

"Payton?" Ned hurried that way. Halfway there, he skidded to a stop as Mickey emerged, rubbing his eyes.

"Hello?" the groom said, sounding sleepy. "What's all the shouting about?"

"Mickey!" I rushed over to him. "Have you seen Payton?"

"Payton?" Mickey blinked at me. "What do you mean? I thought she left with Dana and the others an hour ago."

I pulled out my cell phone and sent Payton a text: WHERE ARE U?

"If everyone else left an hour ago, what are you still doing here?" Ned asked Mickey, sounding suspicious.

Mickey was looking more awake by the second. "I stay here every night," he said. "Extra security. Dana doesn't want to take the chance of anyone messing with the horses overnight."

I couldn't help thinking he wasn't doing such a hot job as an amateur security guard. He hadn't even known Payton was still here.

Unless he's the one who was stalking her, I thought with a shiver.

"Any response yet?" Ned asked, glancing at the phone in my hand.

I shook my head. "Let's check her horses' stalls. Maybe she's in with one of them."

Leaving a confused-looking Mickey behind, we

jogged down the aisle. The first stall we checked contained only a sleepy-looking gray mare.

"Midnight's stall is right over there." I hurried across the aisle and peered inside. "Payton!"

"Nancy!" Payton was leaning against Midnight's side. She straightened up and came to the door. "Thanks for coming. I'm really sorry to bother you guys—Bess told me you were out on a date."

"It's no problem." Ned unclipped the stall guard to let her out. "What happened?"

Payton bit her lip. "I kind of lost track of time and never told Dana I needed a ride," she admitted. "By the time I realized it, everyone was gone."

"You could have called my parents," Ned said. "They'd come get you. Or I would have."

"I know. I was planning to call your dad." Payton glanced at Midnight, who was hanging his head out over the door as if listening to the conversation. "I was just going to say good night to the horses first. I was coming out of Midnight's stall when I saw someone in the aisle."

"Was it Mickey?" I asked.

Payton shook her head. "That's what I thought at first, but it wasn't him. I called out, and instead of answering, the person ran away."

"What did he look like?" I said. "Was it definitely a man?"

"I think so—I'm not sure." Payton bit her lip again. "I really didn't get a good look. It was pretty dark. But it looked like a big guy with broad shoulders. Maybe bald?" She shrugged. "Like I said, it was hard to see, and I guess I wasn't thinking too clearly. . . ."

"It's okay." I put an arm around her shoulders. "Are you sure it wasn't show security or something?"

"I don't think so. Why would a security guard run away as soon as I said something to him?" Payton sounded shaken. "Anyway, I wasn't sure what to do. I was still standing here in the aisle when I heard a weird whistle."

"A whistle?" Ned echoed. "What do you mean?"

"It's hard to describe. It sounded like some kind of—of signal or something, you know? Like in the

~ 136 ~

movies?" Payton let out a low two-note whistle, then shook her head. "I know that sounds crazy."

"Not really," I said. "Not after everything else that's happened around here lately."

She nodded. "Anyway, I was kind of spooked. So I ducked back into Midnight's stall and hid behind him while I texted you."

"I'm glad you did." I glanced at Ned. "Speaking of show security, maybe we should let them know about this. They can keep a lookout for this guy. They might've noticed him entering or leaving the grounds."

"I'll run over to the gate and talk to the guard there," Ned offered. "You guys should probably stay with Mickey until I get back."

"Okay." As he hurried away, Payton and I headed toward the tack room. Mickey was still in the aisle where we'd left him.

"What's going on?" he asked, sounding totally awake by now. "Payton? I didn't know you were here."

"I know, I'm sorry." Payton smiled weakly. "I should have remembered you'd be around and come to find you. Then I wouldn't have had to bother Nancy and Ned."

"It's okay, we really don't mind." I steered her into the tack room and over to a chair. "You should sit down for a minute."

Mickey followed us in, perching on the edge of a cot that was now sitting in the middle of the small room. "Is someone going to tell me what this is all about?"

I filled him in on what Payton had just told me. "Have you seen or heard anything unusual tonight?" I asked.

"Not a thing, sorry." Mickey shot Payton a worried look. "Are you sure it wasn't me you saw?" he asked. "I was pretty tired when I made my rounds last time. Might not have heard you."

"It definitely wasn't you," Payton told the groom with a shaky smile. "This guy was a lot bigger than you. Plus, he definitely reacted when he realized I'd seen him." She glanced at me. "Still, I'm starting to wonder if I panicked for no reason. Maybe it was just some local guy poking around after hours out of curiosity. He might've been as scared as I was."

"What about that weird whistle?" I asked.

"Maybe it was a bird?" She stifled a yawn. "Like I said, I was kind of panicked, so I didn't know what I was hearing at that point."

Just then Ned rushed into the tack room. "Alerted the guards," he said breathlessly. "They'll be on the lookout. Also, Dana just called."

"She called *you*?" Payton asked in surprise.

"Yeah. I guess she's been trying to reach you, but couldn't get an answer."

"Oops." Payton reached into her pocket. "I forgot, I turned off my phone when I hid in Midnight's stall." She looked sheepish. "I was afraid it would ring and give away where I was hiding. So what did Dana want?" She looked apprehensive, and I couldn't blame her. In her current condition, the last thing Payton needed was another scolding from her trainer.

But I felt better when I noticed that Ned was grinning. "She was calling with good news," he said. "She just heard from the show officials or whoever. You guys are in for the Grand Prix tomorrow!"

"What?" Payton looked startled.

"That's great news!" I exclaimed. "So they decided not to suspend?"

"That's right." Ned flopped into another chair. "You guys know how fast Dana talks—I couldn't keep up with all of what she was saying. But I guess the fact that the levels were so low, plus your good reps, made them decide in your favor."

I shot a look at Mickey. The groom looked thoughtful, but his weathered face was difficult to read beyond that. Was he thinking that his plan had failed? I just couldn't tell.

"Wow," Payton said. "I can't believe this."

My attention shifted back to her. "You don't look as thrilled as I thought you'd be," I said. "Aren't you happy that you'll get to ride in the Grand Prix?"

"Sure, of course," Payton said quickly. "It's just that this has all been so crazy, you know?"

"What do you mean?" Ned asked.

Payton sighed. "I feel bad for putting Dana through so much trouble. She likes a drama-free barn—that's why she won't take on just anyone as a client, no matter how talented they are. Like, have you guys ever heard of Cal Kidd?"

"As a matter of fact, we have." I was surprised that she even had to ask. Then I realized I hadn't yet had a chance to mention my suspicions to her. "Um, what about him?"

"I heard he wanted to train with Dana for his big comeback," Payton said. "I guess they've known each other for a long time or something—at least that's what I heard." She added, "But he has kind of a bad rep from his gambling days—too much drama and gossip—so Dana turned him down."

"She did?" This added yet another new wrinkle to things. Could we be looking at this all wrong? Could Cal be our culprit—but trying to punish *Dana* rather than Payton?

"Interesting you should mention Kidd," Mickey spoke up, breaking me out of my thoughts. "I caught him skulking around here last night after hours."

"You did?" I spun to face him. "What happened?"

"Just what I said." The groom shrugged. "I was making the rounds right after everyone left, and saw him hanging around near the feed room. When I asked what he was doing there, Kidd refused to answer and took off."

"Interesting." I shot Ned a meaningful look. "Um, come on, Payton. We'd better get you home."

"Right." Ned clapped Mickey on the shoulder. "Thanks for your help."

"Sure," Mickey murmured, stifling a yawn.

Leaving him to his cot, Ned and Payton and I headed out. Soon we were outside in the cool evening air. Nobody was in sight out there; the only activity was a cat stalking something in the shadow of the next barn.

"That's it, then!" I blurted out. "I bet Cal Kidd is our culprit!"

"Exactly what I was thinking," Ned agreed.

Payton wrinkled her brow. "What are you guys talking about?"

"It all makes sense!" I was feeling excited now. "All

this time we've been thinking the mischief around here has been aimed at you. But it's really been aimed at *Dana*! Cal must be mad at Dana for turning him down, so he's trying to get back at her."

"I don't understand," Payton said, shaking her head. "Most of the stuff hasn't had anything to do with Dana."

"Sure it has. Any sabotage of her star rider could be considered sabotage of her as well." My mind raced as I tried to fit all the pieces together. "And what about those loose horses? We thought whoever let them out was targeting you, because one of them was from Dana's barn and looked a little like Midnight. But maybe the Midnight thing was a coincidence. Maybe the only important thing was that the horse came from Dana's barn."

"But about Midnight . . . ," Ned began.

"I was just getting to that," I said. "The suspension thing works too. Because as Midnight's trainer, Dana was the one who'd pay the price if the horse got suspended. It all makes perfect sense!"

"Okay, I see what you're getting at," Payton said. "And it *would* make perfect sense. Except that everyone on the circuit knows I always sign the entry forms as my own trainer."

That brought me up short. "What?"

Payton nodded. "I sign my own entry forms. There was even an article about it in one of the industry magazines just last month. So I'm sure someone like Cal probably knows about it."

I was struggling to catch up to this new twist. "Wait, but someone told us it's always the trainer who signs," I said.

"Yeah, that's the normal way." Payton glanced at Ned with the ghost of a smile. "But you know my parents don't believe in doing things the normal way. They've always insisted I sign for myself. Dana wasn't thrilled about that at first. In fact, I was afraid that drama might get me kicked out before my first show with Dana."

"I still don't get it," I said. "Why would your parents even care who signs some horse show entry form?"

"I don't know. I guess it's supposed to teach me to be responsible for myself, or more independent, or something," Payton replied. "Just another part of the Evans Edge."

"Can you even do that, though?" Ned wondered. "I mean, you're still a minor."

"You're right, actually my parents have to sign too because of my age," Payton amended. "But in their eyes, *I'm* the one who's ultimately responsible." She glanced at me. "So anyway, this means that even if Midnight had ended up suspended, Dana would have been in the clear. I'm the only one who would've been in trouble."

"Oh." I thought about that for a second. "And you're sure Cal would know about that? You said he's been away from the show scene for a while."

"That doesn't matter," Payton said. "The gambling stuff was only part of the reason Dana didn't want Cal in her barn. The other reason is that he's supposed to be some huge gossip. Trust me, he's got to know."

My shoulders slumped. "Okay, so much for that theory," I muttered. Come to think of it, maybe I'd been too quick to latch onto it anyway. After all, those threatening notes didn't really fit either. Why would someone targeting Dana leave them in such obscure spots, knowing that Payton might not even tell her trainer about them?

Ned stifled a yawn. "Okay, back to the drawing board, I guess," he said. "Maybe we should all head home and sleep on it."

"But what about your date?" Payton sounded worried as we headed toward the parking lot. "I didn't mean to ruin it."

"It's okay, we were almost finished anyway," I said.

"Yeah." Ned grinned at Payton. "Although I was kind of looking forward to dessert. You can make it up to me by giving me half of yours next time our families go out together."

That actually made Payton laugh. "It's a deal."

The next morning I arrived at the show bright and early. Bess and George were with me, though George wasn't particularly happy about it.

"I can't believe people voluntarily wake up this early," she mumbled, stifling a yawn as the three of us walked along the path leading toward Dana's barn.

"Get over it," Bess told her cousin. "The Grand Prix is tonight, and we need to figure out before then who's trying to sabotage Payton."

"That's right," I agreed. "We don't want this hanging over Payton's head on the biggest night of her riding life. Otherwise she might not ride her best in front of the Olympics guy."

"Okay, okay, you're right," George admitted. "So what's the plan?"

"Good question. I can't stop thinking about Cal Kidd," I said.

Bess and George traded a look. I'd filled them in on last night's events on the ride over.

"I thought you ruled that out when you found out Payton signs her own entries," Bess said.

"Right. But here's the thing. What if Cal actually doesn't know she does that?" I kicked at a stone on the path. "Payton seemed convinced that everybody knows, but I'm not sure we should assume anything."

"I suppose it's worth checking into," George said. "So you still think Cal might be getting revenge on Dana?"

"Maybe. I can't stop thinking about what Mickey said about seeing Cal sneaking around the barn the other night. Why would he be there if he's not our culprit?"

"Unless Mickey is lying about that to throw suspicion off himself," Bess suggested.

"Even if it's true, how do you know it's Dana Cal is after?" George put in. "I still think he could be after Payton because of the Midnight connection."

I glanced at her. "You know, I almost forgot about that. Probably because while we were talking about Cal last night, Payton never even mentioned that he used to own Midnight."

"Why would she?" George shrugged. "It's old news, at least to her. But what if it's Cal's real motive? What if he's targeting Payton because he wants his star horse back, and he figures scaring her out of the saddle is the best way to do it?"

"Except that Midnight wasn't his star horse," Bess reminded us. "He wasn't anything special until Payton bought him."

"I still think we should go question Cal," George said. "He's looking like our best suspect either way."

"I've got a better idea." I pointed toward the ring we were passing. "Isn't that Dana over by the rail? Let's go ask her about Cal. At least she should be able to tell us if it's true that he wanted to train with her. And maybe what the deal was with him and Midnight."

We hurried over and joined Dana. She was watching as a stout woman trotted an even stouter horse around the ring.

"Heels down, Sue!" Dana called out. Then she noticed us. "Oh, hello, girls."

"Hi," I said. "We were just wondering something."

Dana didn't seem to hear me. "More impulsion!" she yelled at the woman. "He's moving like a slug, not a horse!"

"Sorry!" the woman's cheerful voice drifted back.

I watched as the rider kicked at the horse's sides.

The horse totally ignored her, trucking along at the same leisurely pace.

Dana sighed, then glanced at us. "What was that?" she said. "Did you girls say something?"

"I wanted to ask you about someone I met yesterday," I said, trying to sound casual. "His name's Cal Kidd."

Dana stiffened. "Cal? What about him?"

"We heard you might know him," George spoke up. "That he might even have wanted to train with you?"

Instead of answering, Dana turned back to face her student. "That's enough for today, Sue!" she hollered. "I've got to go."

"What?" The woman sounded surprised. "But we haven't even warmed up yet!"

"Wait," I said. "I just want to . . ."

I let my voice trail off. It was too late. Dana was already hurrying off without a backward glance.

"Okay, that was weird," George said. "As soon as you mentioned Cal's name, she totally freaked out."

Bess nodded. "So what do we do now?"

I wasn't sure. My phone buzzed, and I answered without bothering to check the caller ID. "Hello?"

"Nancy? Is this Nancy Drew?"

It was a woman's voice I didn't recognize. "Yes, this is Nancy," I said cautiously. "Who's this?"

There was a funny noise from the other end of the line. It sounded like a sob.

I pressed the phone to my ear. "Hello?"

"Nancy!" the voice gasped out again. "This is Annie—Annie Molina? We talked yesterday?"

"Yes, I remember," I said, perplexed.

Annie choked back another sob. "S-sorry to b-bother you," she wailed. "But I had to call someone, and you're the only person at the show whose name I know, and well . . . I just want to confess!"

CHAPTER ELEVEN

The Evans Edge

"THERE SHE IS." GEORGE POINTED OUT through the main gate.

Shading my eyes against the morning sun, I looked that way. Annie Molina was hurrying to meet us. My heart pounded. Could this really be so easy? Was Annie about to solve the case for us by confessing?

"Nancy!" the woman blubbered. She was a mess. Mascara dripped down her splotchy cheeks, and more tears were welling up in her eyes. "I'm so glad I tracked you down. I feel just terrible about all this!"

"Okay," I said. "Why don't you tell us about it?"

Annie nodded, wiping her nose on her sleeve. "I just wanted to help the animals," she said. "And horses are so darling and magical—when I read on PAN's website that they were coming here to protest, I just knew I had to help."

"So this was the first horse show you protested with them?" George asked. "Or was there another one a few weeks or so ago?"

Annie blinked at George as if wondering who she was. "No, this was my first one," she said. "I'd never worked with PAN before. They don't come to this area much."

"But this time they decided to come and protest the River Heights Horse Show," I prompted, poking George in the side to shut her up. I didn't want her questions to confuse Annie, who seemed a little confused already. "So you joined in to try to help the horses."

"That's right." Annie sniffled loudly. "Only I thought we'd just be carrying signs and so forth. It was bad enough when Bill threw that tomato, but then yesterday—oh, dear!" She shuddered.

"Yesterday?" I said.

Annie nodded. "I swear, I only distracted the guard so the others could sneak in," she insisted, the tears starting to flow again. "I didn't even want to do that—the whole plan just seemed too risky—but they convinced me that none of the horses would be hurt!"

"Hold it." I was starting to catch on. "You're talking about those horses getting loose from their stalls, right? Your PAN buddies were the ones who let them out?"

"That's right." Annie pulled a wadded-up tissue out of her pocket and dabbed at her eyes. "Oh, I'm just so glad nothing terrible happened! Even so, I couldn't rest all night. What if one of those beautiful creatures had been hurt? I just couldn't live with myself if we'd caused any real trouble!" She shook her head. "That's not what I thought PAN was all about!"

As far as I knew, that was *exactly* what PAN was all about. But I didn't bother to say so.

"I see," I said. "So what about the other incidents?"

"What other incidents?" Annie looked worried.

"Did something else happen? I just got here myself." She stared wildly around the parking lot.

"So you don't know anything about Payton Evans and her horse's drug test?" Bess put in.

"Who?" Annie said blankly.

Yeah. Maybe Annie wasn't going to solve the case for me after all. All she was confessing to was the loose-horse incident and the tomato throwing.

Just to make sure, we asked her a few more questions. But it soon became clear that we were wasting our time.

After that, it took several minutes to extricate ourselves from Annie's sobbing confession. But finally my friends and I escaped into the show grounds.

"Okay, that was a waste of time," George said as we walked past the snack bar.

"Not really," Bess pointed out. "At least now we know for sure that the tomato thing and the loose horses are red herrings."

I nodded. "And I think we can cross Annie and PAN off the list for the other stuff. It's pretty obvious they're not organized enough to pull off anything too devious."

"Great." George clapped her hands. "Then what are we waiting for? Let's go find our other suspects!"

We spent the next few hours wandering around the show grounds, trying to do just that. Unfortunately, luck seemed to be against us. When we finally located Cal Kidd, he was schooling one of his horses in an out-of-the-way ring. We wasted at least half an hour watching him before giving up and moving on to Lenny Hood. But when we tracked him down, he was surrounded by students—and seemed to be staying that way. As for Dana, she appeared to be actively avoiding us. Was it because of our questions about Cal, or just because she was busy? It was hard to tell.

"This is ridiculous," George said as we leaned on a fence and watched Lenny canter an ornery-looking chestnut over a low fence while the horse's young rider watched from nearby. "The Grand Prix is starting in about an hour, and we haven't made any progress at all!"

"I know." I checked my watch. "Let's go see how Payton's holding up."

Halfway to the barn, we heard shouts coming from behind a shed. Bess looked worried. "That sounds like Dana," she said.

"Exactly what I was thinking." Putting a finger to my lips, I gestured for them to follow as I crept closer to the shed. Dana was still yelling—something about her reputation and how she didn't want to look bad.

". . . and trust me, having you hanging around all the time isn't doing me any favors!" she finished.

By then I was close enough to peek around the edge of the shed. I carefully did so, expecting to see Payton cringing before Dana's fury.

But Payton was nowhere in sight. My jaw dropped when I saw who was facing off against Dana. It was Cal Kidd!

"Whoa!" George breathed in my ear.

I shot her a warning glance. Luckily, Dana hadn't heard a thing. She was glaring at Cal.

"So what do you have to say for yourself?" she demanded.

"I don't know why you're so mad at me," Cal said

in a surly tone. "I'm the one who should be mad. I mean, what kind of person won't even help out her own brother when he needs a hand?"

"*Half* brother," Dana snapped. "And as usual, you're not listening to me. I don't care if we're family—I'm not going to be your shortcut back into the show world. Not until you prove to me that you've cleaned up your act for good." She poked a finger in his face. "And bad-mouthing Payton all over the place isn't helping your cause. I don't care *how* badly she beats you in every class!"

I stepped back, pushing my friends with me. My head was spinning with what I'd just heard.

"I can't believe this," Bess exclaimed once we were safely away. "Dana and Cal are brother and sister?"

"*Half* brother and sister," George corrected. "And now that she mentions it, I can sort of see the family resemblance."

I didn't say anything for a second. What did this mean? As far as I could tell, it just added one more wrinkle to an already rumpled and confusing case.

"Do you think they could be in cahoots?" I wondered at last.

"Dana and Cal?" Bess shrugged. "Maybe."

George glanced back toward the shed. "Although they didn't sound too chummy just now," she added. "Dana actually seemed upset that Cal doesn't like Payton."

"This probably explains why Cal was hanging around Dana's stalls the other night," I mused. "And why he wouldn't tell Mickey what he was doing there. He must've been trying to catch Dana alone to try to talk her into training him or whatever."

"So you don't think he has anything to do with our case?" Bess asked.

"I didn't say that. We *did* see him freak out after Payton did so well in that jumper class they were both in. And there's still the Midnight connection." I rubbed my forehead as if trying to jump-start my brain. The more information we got, the more muddled this case seemed.

We continued to discuss it as we resumed our walk.

Unfortunately, we didn't reach any new conclusions, and by the time we neared Dana's barn, I was feeling frustrated. Why couldn't I figure this one out? I had several distinct and troubling incidents, several promising suspects. But none of the pieces fit together!

When we reached Dana's section of the barn, we saw a horse cross-tied in the aisle. Jen was hard at work currying the animal's already spotless gray coat.

"Hi," I said as we reached her. "Have you seen Payton lately?"

The young groom looked up with a smile. "I think I saw her go into the tack stall," she said, gesturing with the curry comb she was holding. "She's probably getting ready to tack up for the Grand Prix."

"Thanks." I led the way toward the tack stall.

"You're not planning to talk to Payton about the case, are you, Nancy?" Bess asked as soon as we were out of the groom's earshot. "Because she probably needs to focus right now with the Grand Prix coming up so soon."

I frowned, realizing she was right. "Okay, we'll just wish her luck and then leave her alone." I sighed. "At this point it's probably too late to solve this before the Grand Prix anyway."

"That's the spirit," George joked.

I was rolling my eyes at her as we stepped into the tack stall. Out of the corner of one of those rolling eyes, I saw Payton bent over a saddle rack. She jerked back in surprise and straightened up when she heard us.

"Oh!" she exclaimed. "You startled me."

"Sorry." Noticing that she was holding a pocket-knife with the blade open, I glanced at the rack in front of her. It held a saddle with a white pad and leather girth slung over the seat. "What are you doing?"

"Nothing," she said, reaching over to fiddle with the pad. Then she glanced at the knife. "I mean, I was just scraping some dried mud off my backup saddle, since my regular one got ruined. Dana doesn't like seeing dirty tack, especially in the bigger classes." She smiled weakly, then snapped the knife shut.

"Speaking of your ruined saddle, where did that knife come from?" Bess stared at it. "Did you leave it anywhere that someone could find it?"

Realizing what she was driving at, I shot her a smirk. "I thought we weren't going to bug Payton about the case before her big class, detective," I joked.

"Sorry, you're right," Bess said quickly. "Don't pay any attention to me, Payton."

"No, it's okay." Payton smiled uncertainly. "Um, this isn't my knife. I just borrowed it from one of the grooms. They all keep them around to cut hay twine and stuff."

That made sense. "So whoever slashed your other saddle probably didn't have any trouble finding a knife to do it with." I shook my head. "Just one more clue that's not as useful as it seems, I guess."

Just then Jen stuck her head into the room. "Payton," she said. "Dana just texted me to see where you are. She wants to start warming you and Midnight up in ten minutes. Should I text Mickey so he can come help you tack up?"

"No thanks, I've got it. Tell Dana I'm on my way." Grabbing the saddle and other stuff off the rack, Payton headed for the door.

"Good luck!" my friends and I called in unison.

"Thanks!" She tossed us one last smile, then disappeared.

Bess perched on the edge of a tack trunk. "We should probably find Ned and then grab seats for the Grand Prix before it gets crowded."

"Yeah." George sounded distracted. She bent down and picked something up from under the empty saddle rack Payton had been using. "Hey, no fair!" she complained, holding up an empty candy wrapper. "Payton was eating a Chocominto bar and didn't share!"

I grinned. Chocomintos were George's favorite candy. "Too bad for you," I said. "But how do you know it was even Payton who dropped that wrapper? We didn't see her eating any candy. She didn't even have chocolate smeared around her mouth like you always get when you pig out on those things."

George made a face at me. "You know, sometimes having a detective for a friend is a real drag." Tossing the candy wrapper into the trash bin in the corner, she headed for the door. "Let's go. I want to make sure we have good seats for the Grand Prix."

···

"Wow," Ned said. "So Dana and Cal are related? That's wild."

"Shh. It seems to be some kind of secret—I don't think even Payton knows." I glanced around to make sure nobody had overheard. Luckily, the people sitting in the stands around us were all focused on their own conversations. Everyone seemed excited for the start of the Grand Prix.

The bleachers set up around the main ring were crowded and getting more so every minute. My friends and I had arrived early enough to snag seats in the second row, which gave us a spectacular view of the course. The huge, colorful jumps had actually taken my mind off the case for a few minutes. There were brightly colored rails, a fake brick wall, even a pair of jump standards shaped like riverboats in honor of our town's riverside heritage.

"It's hard to believe someone we know is actually going to jump a horse over those, huh?" Bess said, her gaze wandering to the jumps.

"Yeah." I shivered with anticipation. "I just hope Payton isn't distracted by everything that's happened." I glanced around, wondering where the Olympic chef d'équipe was sitting.

"Payton seems like a pretty cool customer when it comes to competing," George said. "I'm sure she'll be fine."

"Still, I wish we could've figured out this case before now." I sighed.

"Me too," Ned agreed. Bess, George, and I had just finished filling him in on everything that had happened that day—not that there was much to tell. "So back to Cal—if he's Dana's brother, does this mean he's off the suspect list?"

"No way," George said. "He might still want Midnight back. What better way to make a big splash in his return to show jumping than by riding a star horse? There's your motive right there. And Cal definitely had the opportunity to do most of the bad stuff, since nobody would think twice about seeing him around the barn. He could've easily slipped something into Midnight's feed bucket. And slashed Payton's saddle, too."

"So could Lenny Hood," I said. "Or Jessica Watts. Or Dana herself. Or Mickey." I shook my head. "The thing that keeps bugging me is those threatening notes—especially the second one."

"What do you mean?" Bess asked.

"I mean, I can see how most of our suspects might be able to figure out which car belonged to Payton's family and leave a note there." I glanced around at my friends. "But how in the world would any of them know she was staying at Ned's—or that she'd ever find a note left inside the beat-up old grill at his house?"

"Don't let my dad hear you talk about Bertha that way," Ned joked. Then his expression went serious again. "But actually, that's a good point, Nancy."

"Maybe someone at the show overheard us talking about the barbecue," Bess suggested.

"I suppose it's possible. Although that makes it more likely to be Dana or Mickey, right? Do you remember seeing either of them hanging around while we were talking about the barbecue?" I asked.

George shrugged. "I don't even remember when we mentioned the barbecue."

Just then the crowd roared as the first rider entered the ring. "It's starting," Ned said. "We'll have to talk about this later."

For the next half hour, I did my best to focus on the action. The Grand Prix was exciting, but I couldn't help feeling distracted. Why couldn't I crack this case? There had to be something I was missing. . . .

I tuned back in when I heard the crowd gasp. An older male rider on a fractious black horse had just knocked down the top pole on a jump. Another jump was coming up fast, and the horse was racing forward with its head straight up in the air, looking completely out of control. Sure enough, it veered sideways as it approached the next obstacle, a large, solid-looking jump with a pair of fake stone columns as standards.

"Oh!" I exclaimed along with everyone else as the horse crashed sideways into one of the columns, sending it flying. The horse stumbled over a pole and almost went down. The rider came off, hitting the ground hard and rolling out of the way of his mount's flying hooves.

"Yikes," Bess said. "I hope the rider's okay."

"He's already getting up." I clutched the edge of my seat and leaned forward, my gaze shifting back to the horse. It leaped over the scattered poles and glanced off the other standard, knocking that one over as well. Then it started galloping wildly around the ring, reins and stirrups flying, veering around the people who hurried in to try to catch it. Everyone gasped again as the horse headed for one of the other jumps, leaping over it wildly and knocking down a couple of more poles.

George squinted down toward the in-gate. "Check it out, there's Payton. Let's hope Midnight doesn't see that other horse and get any ideas, huh?"

I turned to look. Payton was riding Midnight toward the gate. The big gelding looked magnificent—his bay coat gleamed, set off by his crisp white saddle pad. Dana was scurrying along beside the horse, talking a mile a minute, though we were way too far away to hear what she was saying.

Payton halted a few steps from the gate, watching with everyone else as the people in the ring finally caught the black horse. Meanwhile Dana stepped toward Midnight's midsection, her hand reaching to move Payton's leg aside. But Payton nudged her trainer's hand away with her boot, then swung the horse aside and leaned forward from the saddle, slipping her own hand under the girth. I was too far away to see clearly, but I was pretty sure Dana had a frown on her face, though she stepped back as Payton straightened up again.

My friends were watching too. "What was that all about?" Ned wondered.

"Dana was trying to double-check that the girth is tight enough, I think," I said. "When I was a kid, my riding teacher used to do that before I rode. It's a safety thing—you don't want the girth to be too loose, or your saddle might slip."

"I guess Payton wanted to check it herself," Bess said. "Maybe she's still mad at Dana from that blowup we overheard yesterday."

"I wouldn't blame her," George put in.

"Maybe that's it." I frowned slightly as I glanced from Payton to Dana. "Or maybe there's a reason Payton doesn't trust Dana when it comes to her safety equipment."

Ned shot me a worried look. "Do you think so?"

"It might be worth asking Payton about later," I answered thoughtfully.

"Hey, Ned, here come your parents." Bess pointed.

Ned stood for a better look. "Payton's folks are with them," he said. "That's good—Mom was afraid their plane would be delayed and they'd miss Payton's big moment."

Cupping his hands around his mouth, he called out to his parents, then waved so they could see where he was sitting. Moments later, the Nickersons and Payton's parents were squeezing in beside us. Mr. Evans was a big man with a booming laugh, while Dr. Evans was petite and delicate-looking like her daughter.

"Made it in the nick of time!" Dr. Evans exclaimed, peering down at the ring.

Mr. Nickerson nodded. "Looks like Payton's on deck."

"Right," I said, glancing out at the ring. The black horse was gone, and Payton was riding in. She started walking Midnight around at the end of the ring as the crew reassembled the jumps the black horse had knocked over.

"She's looking good, isn't she?" Mr. Evans said. "Focused. Strong."

"You must be very proud of her," I said with a smile. "It's amazing that she's competing at this level at her age. That Evans Edge stuff is really working!"

Payton's father chuckled. "She told you about that, eh?"

"Uh-huh. She seems to take it pretty seriously." I couldn't help thinking that a certain aspect of the Evans Edge had almost ended up causing her to be suspended from competing. "Especially the part about signing her own paperwork at the shows instead of having Dana do it."

"Oh, that." Mr. Evans rolled his eyes. "Yeah, that's a pain in the neck if you ask me—it means I've had to fax my signature to every dang show for the past three or four months, since she can't legally sign on her own yet." He smiled and shook his head. "Still, once Payton gets an idea in her head, there's no changing her mind."

His wife heard him and chuckled. "Yes, I wonder where she got that from?" she quipped, reaching over to squeeze her husband's hand.

"Wait a minute," I said, a little confused. "You mean signing as her own trainer was *Payton's* idea? But I thought she said—"

"Look!" Ned exclaimed, cutting me off. "Payton's starting!"

While I was talking with Mr. Evans, the crew had finished rebuilding the jumps. We all watched as Payton finally nudged her horse into a relaxed trot, beginning a big, loopy circle around part of the ring. From watching previous rounds, I knew she was waiting for the buzzer to sound so she could begin.

I glanced over at Mr. Evans, who was chatting with Bess. Why was his last comment bugging me so much? Okay, so Payton put as much pressure on herself as her parents did. That was obvious. It didn't have anything to do with the case—did it?

My mind sorted through the clues and incidents again, looking for patterns. Any of our suspects could be the culprit—right? Except I kept getting stuck on that note in the grill. I tried to picture Lenny Hood following Payton home from the show grounds, then sneaking into the Nickersons' backyard. Or Jessica. Or Cal or Dana or Mickey.

It just didn't compute. How on earth would any of them pull it off? Perhaps more important, *why* would any of them hide a note in such an out-of-the-way place?

There was only one logical answer. They wouldn't. That meant somebody else must have done it.

I glanced over at Dr. Evans and Mrs. Nickerson, who had their heads close together as they chattered and laughed while waiting for Payton's round to start. A new idea crept into my mind. Could it be . . . ?

The buzzer sounded, startling me out of my thoughts.

"Here she goes!" Mr. Evans exclaimed as Payton cantered Midnight around to the end of the ring, picking up speed as she aimed him toward the timer flags.

There was a loud whoop from down by the gate. Glancing that way, I saw Dana standing there, watching Payton.

I gasped as the answer hit me like a horse's hoof to the gut. "Stop!" I shouted, leaping out of my seat so fast I almost tripped over Bess. "Stop her!"

"Nancy!" Mrs. Nickerson cried. "What are you doing?"

The others were gasping and crying out too, but I ignored them. I lunged down the bleachers, almost stepping on the hand of the man sitting in front of me.

"Stop her!" I yelled as loudly as I could, waving both hands over my head. "Please! You have to stop this round!"

CHAPTER TWELVE

Driven

I RACED FOR THE RING, IGNORING THE shouts and stares from people around me. I had to stop Payton before it was too late.

There were too many people between me and the gate, so I pushed aside some spectators standing at the fence and vaulted over. I was vaguely aware of people running toward me—jump crew, probably, trying to stop the crazy girl from ruining the show—but I had a head start as I dashed across the ring. Midnight was just a few strides out from the first jump on the course, his ears pricked forward. Was I already too late?

"No!" I howled, pushing my legs to pump faster.

Payton heard me and glanced over. A look of confusion crossed her face as she saw me running toward her.

Midnight heard me coming too. He spooked away from me, losing speed as he lurched sideways.

"Go!" Payton urged, kicking the horse to get him moving again.

But the horse's hesitation had given me the time I needed. I threw myself forward, grabbing for the reins. Midnight tossed his head, almost dragging me off my feet. But I held on, and the horse came to a prancing, snorting halt.

"Nancy, what are you doing?" Payton's face was very pale beneath her black riding helmet. "Let go!"

I met her eye, not backing off. "You don't have to do this, you know."

Someone grabbed my shoulder from behind. "Come with me, young lady," a gruff voice said.

Glancing back, I saw a particularly burly member of the jump crew. A man in a suit was hurrying toward me as well—some sort of official, I assumed.

"Get her out of here," the official snapped. He glanced up at Payton. "I'm sorry about this, Ms. Evans. If you need a moment to regroup or settle your horse, of course it's no problem."

"What's going on?" Dana demanded, rushing over to us. "Payton, are you okay?" Without waiting for an answer, she whirled to glare at me. "What in the world are you doing?" She shoved me back away from Midnight and grabbed his reins herself, running her free hand down the horse's neck soothingly. Then she glanced at the jump-crew guy. "Get her out of here already!"

"Wait." I resisted as the guy started to pull me away. "Look at this, Dana."

Slipping out of the man's grasp, I stepped forward and slid my hand under the girth, giving it a hard yank.

SNAP! It broke apart just under the saddle flap. The loose end flopped down against Midnight's front legs, making him jump in surprise.

"Whoa!" Dana exclaimed, her eyes going wide with alarm as Payton's saddle, suddenly left with nothing but gravity holding it on the horse's back, slipped to one side. "Easy, boy . . ."

I stepped back, shoulders slumping. My hunch had been right. I sort of wished it hadn't been.

Dana managed to keep Midnight still long enough for Payton to slide down before the saddle could slip any further. Then the trainer grabbed the girth for a closer look, her expression going grim as she examined it.

"It looks like this girth was cut almost all the way through. If it had broken while Payton was going over a jump . . . But how did this happen?" she blustered. "I always check all tack myself before my clients go in for—oh. Wait." She shot Payton a confused look. "Except this time I didn't . . ."

"Let's get out of here," I urged, suddenly aware of the murmurs of the crowd as they watched. "We don't need an audience for this." Noticing that the jump-crew guy was moving toward me again, I gulped. "Um, Dana, can you tell them to back off? Please? I can explain."

Dana frowned at me, seeming undecided for a second. Finally she shrugged. "It's okay," she told the men. "I'll sort it out and let you know if we need help."

By the time we got out of the ring, my friends, the Nickersons, and Payton's parents were waiting for us. "What happened?" Dr. Evans cried, wrapping her daughter in a hug.

"Oh my gosh, Payton!" Bess exclaimed at the same time. "If your girth had broken over the top of one of those huge jumps, you could've been killed!"

George was staring at me. "Nancy, how did you know that was going to happen?"

"Because I finally figured out who's behind everything that's been happening," I said.

Ned gasped. "You mean the same person who drugged Midnight and slashed Payton's saddle did this, too? Messed with her girth so she'd fall off?"

"That's cold!" George shot Dana a suspicious glance. "So who was it?"

"Not any of the people you're thinking of." I turned and gave Payton a meaningful look.

She met my eye, her lower lip trembling slightly. Then she nodded and squared her shoulders.

"It was me," she said. "I did it. All of it."

"What?" several voices exclaimed at once.

"That's right. I messed up my girth, and my saddle, too." Payton took a deep breath. "And I fed Midnight chocolate to make him flunk that drug test."

Dana looked grim. "Payton, you're the *last* person I ever thought would cheat to give yourself an edge."

"That's not why I did it!" Payton protested quickly. She pulled off her helmet. "Please, just let me explain." She shot her parents an unreadable look.

"Payton?" her father prompted. "What's this about?"

"I just wanted a break, you know?" Payton blurted out. Her eyes filled with tears. "From the pressure, the need to be the best at all costs. From not having a life outside of showing. From always being afraid I was going to let someone down." She paused. "And especially from feeling like I was pushing my horses way too hard. Especially this guy."

Midnight had turned his head to stare at the ring as another horse-and-rider pair entered. At Payton's touch, he turned and nuzzled her hair, the rings of his bit clanking against her head.

There was a babble of voices, some confused and some angry, as everyone reacted to Payton's revelation. I ignored them, watching Payton.

"So you decided to frame yourself," I said. "Make everyone think you were in danger so they'd let you quit. Maybe even *insist* you quit."

Payton ran her fingers lightly over Midnight's face. "That wasn't my first plan," she said. "First I tried to get myself suspended. I've been slipping chocolate to any of my horses that'll eat it for months."

"Ever since you first started signing as your own trainer?" I guessed.

She nodded. "I definitely didn't want Dana to get in trouble. . . ."

After that, the words poured out of her like water out of a broken dam. At first she'd been willing to wait however long it took for one of her "drugged" horses to be selected for random drug testing. But then the chef d'équipe had announced that he was coming to the River Heights show—and Payton's parents and Dana insisted that Payton skip her cousin's wedding to attend.

That had made Payton desperate enough to plant that note on her father's car. That hadn't done the trick either, obviously. Payton ended up in River Heights anyway. Even so, she'd decided to do whatever it took to avoid riding in front of the chef d'équipe, which she seemed to see as the point of no return. First she'd called in that anonymous tip to the stewards about herself. Then she'd sneaked the second note into the grill, hoping that when Mrs. Nickerson saw it, she'd put pressure on her old friend to pull Payton from the show.

That didn't work either, so next Payton slashed her own saddle. She tried calling Ned and me, pretending a shadowy man was stalking her. She even let the news about Midnight's drug test slip to Jessica Watts, know-ing the gossip would be all over the show grounds in a heartbeat, which Payton hoped would influence the decision of the officials.

But when even the long-awaited failed drug test failed to stop her from reaching the Grand Prix ring, Payton had really panicked.

"I didn't want to hurt Midnight," she said, still stroking her horse's neck. "So I figured it was going to have to be me."

Dr. Evans gasped. "Oh, Payton . . ."

"So that's what you were doing when we came into the tack room earlier," George said. "You weren't cleaning dirt off your saddle with that knife. You were using it to slice through your girth."

Payton nodded. "You guys almost caught me."

Mr. Evans looked grim. "I wish you'd come to us about all of this, Payton."

"I'm sorry, Daddy," Payton whispered. She looked around at all of us, her gaze finally settling on Dana. "I'm really, really sorry. For everything."

Dana looked uncertain. "Payton . . ."

"Will you take Midnight back to the barn for me?"

Payton asked her trainer. "Please? I left some carrots for him in my tack trunk." She stroked the horse's face one more time. "No more Chocomintos for you, buddy."

Mr. Evans turned to face me. "Thank you for stopping her, young lady," he said. "I—we—really appreciate it. If she'd gone through with her crazy plan . . ." His voice trailed off as he glanced at his daughter with a hint of uncertainty in his eyes. "Well, thanks. Now if you'll all excuse us, I think it's time we had a serious family talk."

"Are you sure you're not in the mood for brunch?" I poked my head into my father's home office. "I could call and see if they have a table for us at that little café on River Street. You love that place."

Dad glanced up from his computer. "Sorry, Nancy," he said. "I already told you, I've got to get through these briefs before tomorrow."

I frowned, feeling restless. That often happened after I wrapped up a tough case. Not that this one felt very wrapped up. Sure, I'd figured out who was behind all the mischief. But what was going to happen with Payton's riding career now? That remained a mystery.

"Well, maybe I'll just go out for a run, then," I said, turning away.

"Wait," Dad said. I spun around, hoping my father had changed his mind about brunch. But he was frowning slightly. "Actually, would you mind tossing a load into the washer? I'm all out of clean socks, and since it's Hannah's day off today . . ."

I sighed loudly. It was a beautiful day, and I wasn't in the mood for laundry. Still, Dad rarely asked me to pitch in with extra housework, since our housekeeper, Hannah Gruen, took care of most of it. So I didn't feel right saying no.

"Sure," I said. "I'll go take care of it right now."

I trudged upstairs to grab the hamper. The doorbell rang when I was halfway back down the stairs.

"I'll get it!" I shouted in the general direction of Dad's office. Hurrying over to the front door, I swung it open. "Payton!" I blurted out in surprise.

Payton smiled at me. "Hi, Nancy," she said. "Hope

you don't mind me stopping by without calling first."

"No, not at all." I stepped aside. "Would you like to come in?"

"Actually, I was wondering if you wanted to go for a ride." Payton waved a hand at the car parked by the curb. "My parents are letting me use their rental car, and I could use a change of scenery. And someone to talk to."

"Sure. Let me grab my purse."

Soon we were on the road. I wasn't sure where Payton was heading, and I didn't ask. It didn't really matter.

"So I wanted to say thanks," Payton said as she eased the car to a stop at a traffic light. "I mean, at first I was kind of mad at you for stopping me. But it was the right thing to do." She shot me a look. "I guess I went a little crazy."

"I understand," I said. "And you're welcome."

She drove across the intersection as the light turned green. "Anyway, my mom calls what I did a 'cry for help.' I think that means she thinks I wanted to get caught." She shook her head. "I just couldn't think of another way to get my parents' attention—to convince them to let me slow down. They don't believe in giving up on anything they start."

"The Evans Edge," I murmured.

She nodded. "Right. That edge can be sharp, I guess. Anyway, they're paying attention now. I think they're starting to understand how I feel. Or at least trying."

"So they're going to let you give up showing?"

"If that's what I want." Payton hesitated. "I'm not sure if I want to give it up for good. I mean, I used to love it."

She glanced out the side window. We were heading out of town by now, passing by larger properties and small farms. Horses were grazing in some of the fields we were passing.

"Giving up showing doesn't mean giving up horses, does it?" I asked.

"That's exactly what I've been thinking," Payton said. "I think I'm going to take a break from competition and try just riding for fun for a while. See if I can remember what I used to love about it."

She hit the turn signal. There was no intersection in sight—just an unmarked gravel driveway.

"Where are we going?" I asked.

"You'll see." She smiled as she spun the wheel to turn into the driveway.

I glanced down the lane. It ended at a cute little red barn. Was Payton planning to start rediscovering the joy of riding right now?

Payton brought the car to a stop near the barn. "Look!" she said.

I looked where she was pointing. My jaw dropped as a gorgeous horse and carriage came into view. A woman I didn't recognize was holding the reins. Sitting beside her was someone I *definitely* recognized.

"Ned!" I blurted out.

Payton grinned. "Surprise!"

"What? But I don't understand . . . ," I began.

"It's your anniversary gift," she explained as we both climbed out of the car. "Dana knows the woman who owns this place. I know I ruined your dinner the other night, and Ned mentioned that it was originally supposed to be a picnic. So I figured I'd help him arrange a nice, romantic makeup picnic today."

"Oh!" Suddenly something else made a lot more sense. "Wait—was my dad in on this too, by any chance? Was that why he wouldn't let me leave the house?"

Payton nodded, still grinning. "Don't worry, she's definitely surprised," she called to Ned proudly as we approached the carriage.

"Impressive. It's not easy to pull one over on River Heights's greatest young sleuth." Ned winked at her.

I laughed. "Yeah, you got me," I admitted. "And I love it!"

Payton stepped over to pat the horse, a stocky palomino with a sweet face. "Well, what are you waiting for, Nancy? Your carriage awaits!"

"Thanks, Payton." I smiled at her, glad to see real happiness in her face as she patted the horse. I hoped she would be able to rediscover the joy in riding—and maybe even in showing. Considering some of the characters I'd met over the past few days, I had a feeling the show circuit needed as many people like her as possible.

But I wasn't going to focus on that right now. I took the hand Ned was offering me, climbing up into the carriage.

"Ready to ride off into the sunset with me?" Ned asked, squeezing my hand. "Or at least the midday sun?"

I squeezed back. "I'm ready."

Dear Diary

POOR PEYTON.

The pressure she was under to perform and be number one was too much for her. It would have been too much for anybody, really. It's too bad she just couldn't talk to her parents and tell them how she truly felt.

But harming Midnight sure wasn't the answer.

Hurting anybody—or anything—never is.

READ WHAT HAPPENS IN THE NEXT MYSTERY
IN THE NANCY DREW DIARIES,

Once Upon a Thriller

AS WE HEADED OUT TO THE CAR, GEORGE and I quickly filled Bess in on what she had missed.

"Weird!" Bess exclaimed. "What do you think 'nine-one-fourteen' means?"

"I don't know," I replied. "Some sort of a code? A date?"

"September first, 2014," George stated matter-of-factly.

"Could be," I mused.

We drove back to the cabin in silence, mulling it

over. Then we unloaded our groceries and put everything in the fridge, put on our bathing suits, shorts, and tank tops, and headed outside. Bess unlocked the equipment shed near the cabin, and retrieved the paddles while George and I carried the canoe down to the tiny stretch of rocky sand just behind our cabin.

Bess pulled a bright orange life vest over her head, then handed one each to George and me.

"Ugh," she sighed. "Why do they have to make these so ugly?"

"So they can be spotted in a storm," I replied simply.

"Thanks, supersleuth," Bess joked. "It was a rhetorical question, though."

She squinted at the sky as she donned her life vest. "Speaking of storms, it looks a little dark off in the distance, doesn't it?" she asked. "Maybe we should wait until tomorrow to take out the canoe."

She was right—the sky above the horizon was definitely gray. I pulled out my phone to check the weather.

"Well, there's no rain predicted for this afternoon,"

I assured her. "I think we should be okay. And I'm really curious to check out Lacey O'Brien's cabin."

"I'm not sure I agree, but all right," Bess grumbled. George just shrugged and followed us down to the shore. We climbed into the canoe and pushed off. As George and Bess paddled, I looked around at the many different green shades of the trees next to deep blue of the water. It should have been soothing scenery, but it wasn't.

I couldn't turn off my brain.

"Stop fidgeting, Nancy. What are you thinking about anyway?" Bess asked.

"Just the bookstore fire," I replied. "I'm really curious to hear what the fire department says. Paige seemed awfully certain it was accidental, but I'm not so sure. And she seemed so jumpy when I picked up that slip of paper. And where was Lacey O'Brien's this morning. I know she's a recluse, but why didn't she shown up for her book signing?"

Bess nodded. "Good questions."

I continued. "And what about Alice Ann? I

overheard her talking to the baker in front of the Cheshire Cat before I bought the books, and she didn't seem particularly fond of Paige or Lacey."

"Wait, who's Alice Ann?" George asked. She handed the paddle to me as we carefully switched places.

"That woman at the inn who returned my wallet and gave us directions to Lacey O'Brien's cabin," I explained as I started paddling.

"Oh, right," George answered. Then she glanced down at her phone, which was open to a compass app. "Speaking of directions, that's the northwest corner of the lake right there."

George looked from her phone back up at the gray sky.

"I'm wondering if maybe we should turn back, though," she said worriedly. "It's gotten a lot darker and my hair's suddenly standing on end because of all the static electricity in the air. I don't like the idea of being on the water in a lightning storm, no matter who we're looking for."

"I agree," Bess said nervously. "And the wind is

changing—I can feel it. I'm getting goose pimples on my arms."

The sky definitely did look more menacing than it had before, but suddenly I caught a glimpse of a dark figure on the beach.

"Look!" I cried out. "Over there on the beach. You think it's Lacey O'Brien?"

I gave George and Bess a pleading look.

"We're actually closer to this shore of the lake now than we are to our cabin," George said with a sigh. "I'd rather be near the shore—any shore—than in the middle of the lake if we do run into trouble."

"Maybe . . ." I began. "Maybe we can land on the beach there and ask for some temporary shelter if it starts to storm."

Bess sighed.

"You're both right," she agreed. "But next time you'll listen to me. Turning back now would be more dangerous than going ashore here."

Bess and I paddled hard. The gusts picked up while George gripped the sides of the canoe. The wind was whipping at us from every direction, but there was nothing else to do but press on.

The shadowy figure on the shore loomed larger as we got closer. I put my head down and used all my strength as I pulled on the paddle. The waves were getting bigger, and every time one hit us we rocked unsteadily from side to side.

"Whoa!" Bess cried out.

"Ugh," George moaned. "This rocking motion is making me feel ill."

"Try to keep the canoe cutting through the water perpendicular to the waves!" I called to Bess over the howling wind. "That way we won't tip over."

"Okay!" Bess called back as she and I both maneuvered to turn the canoe so the bow of the boat was slicing through the waves at a right angle. Suddenly the wind changed and a swell of water hit us hard from the left, causing us to tip toward the right.

"Yikes!" Bess screamed. At that moment George pointed to a floating dock that had come up seemingly out of nowhere.

"Nancy! Bess!" she shouted. "Watch out!"

In trying not to hit the dock, Bess and I managed to turn the canoe so that we were once again parallel to the waves. A second later, we were hit from the left with another giant swell.

Before I even realized what was happening, the boat lurched wildly to the right, throwing us into the dark, churning water.